THE TRUTH IN THE DARK

A GINNIE HARPER STATICPUNK MYSTERY
BOOK 1

BRITNEY DEHNERT

Britney Dehnert
BOOKS

AUTHOR'S NOTE

The staticpunk world is an alternate history world much like cyberpunk or steampunk, where the technology is the focus of contrast between the "punk" world and our own. In staticpunk, the key change is the rise of a fictional apprentice of Nikola Tesla's: Yuri Morislav. His inventions and idealism center on wireless technology that exceed the genius of our own 1890-1930s. We invite you now to this world, a world that looks at electricity and innovation in a completely different way…

In 1890, a young and wealthy manufacturer named Edward Baughmann saw Morislav's potential and invested heavily in him, especially encouraging his inventions that others saw as outlandish or farfetched. Morislav's genius combined with Baughmann's riches and marketing expertise rocketed Morislav's patents into mass production, ushering in an era of technology marked by his ingenuity. Together they built a new production company on the American east coast near Baughmann's hometown, the Park, a quiet village populated mostly by old money. The company attracted workers for miles around, and soon, a large city developed around Morislav Co.

Morislav himself, inspired by the glow surrounding him on the street one foggy night, christened the city Luxity, a city filled with light, and the name took hold. By the 1920s, Morislav is a household name, and his inventions are societal staples.

Ginnie Harper is a reporter for the *Franklin Journal* in this world.

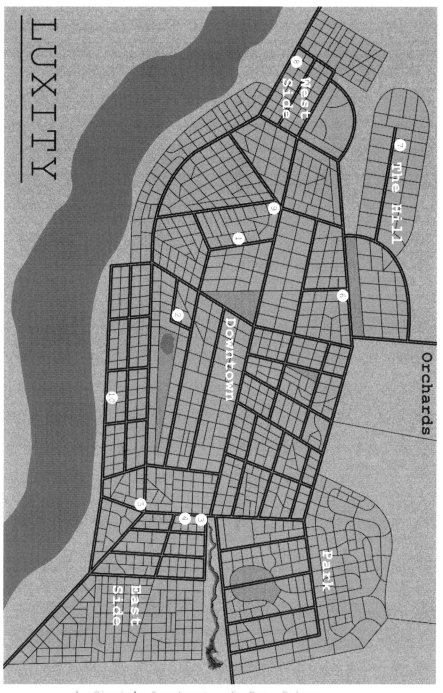

LUXITY

West Side

The Hill

7

9

1

6

Downtown

2

10

Orchards

5

4

3

East Side

Park

1. Ginnie's Apartment
2. Franklin Journal
3. Tulip Haven
4. Lily Bed
5. Dahlia's Delights

6. Rose Palace
7. Baughmann's Home
8. Vangees Appliances
9. Mel's Diner
10. Construction Site

1

I am putting pen to paper now, though my candle flickers and grows weak, because the story stands too vividly in my mind. I cannot sleep or eat, and I think it is because I must write. For now, all the details are strong in my memory, and I cannot rest until I ensure the record remains true. You see, the events have just concluded. The case is closed. But the hurt still pounds in my chest, the ache has not left, and perhaps by writing everything — everything — on paper, I may learn how to move on, how to slip back into my life that I love. For I really do love my life, the life that I chose for myself, not too terribly long ago.

My name is Eugenia, Eugenia Olivia Harper. Those three names are the ones that I chose to keep after I left my family in their five story peak-top on Golden Maple Lane and moved into this little apartment on the other side of Luxity, on Starling Street. Most of my acquaintances here don't even know my last name: most of them simply call me Ginnie. Sometimes I smile, hearing the colloquial nickname sung after me as a fellow journalist runs up with a message or as my boss (heaven help me) thunders the simple syllables from his office upstairs. I chuckle sometimes because I remember the way

Eugenia rolled delicately off my Mother's magenta-stained lips, or the way Father called for me when he returned home from the city.

"Eugenia! Eugenia Olivia Candace Harper Elizabeth Jefferson!"

It almost sounds like a yodel when strung together like that.

But no more. No, usually I'm just Ginnie Harper, first floor reporter at the *Franklin Journal*, and I don't miss the china plates or lace petticoats (I can see my mother's horrified face at the callousness of putting the word 'petticoat' on paper!) or afternoons spent sitting on a cushion embroidering.

I do miss the piano.

The first purchase I made with my new wage at the *Journal* that was not bread or eggs was a pretty little keyed instrument I slipped off the shelf at Bergman's Pawn Shop and bargained for with the best dead-eyed, uninterested look that I've ever manufactured, all the while dying to have it. Either my acting was a success or the proprietor knew he'd never sell such an instrument in this part of the city, but either way, I got it home, and somehow I've loved it more fiercely than I ever did my great, mahogany, room-filling piano-grand. It's not too loud for my apartment, and needing to warm up its little mechanism first makes me appreciate the sweet little timbre it offers when I finally begin to play. The piano-miniature's gentle tone got me through the days after I was assigned my first murder story. It was a rather gruesome killing (I still think Mac assigned me to it to see if this medium-stature, prim-dressing, high-society "girl" could handle the rigors of the scandals we report to the public), and I spent about a month afterwards with bags under my eyes, pretending that I didn't stay up most of the night playing piano instead of sleeping with the threat of horrendous nightmares. Gene had to bump my elbow and clear his throat loudly to jolt me awake during the evening staff meetings, but no one else seemed to notice. Thankfully, he was discreet enough to keep it our little secret.

I never meant to tell anyone at the *Journal* of my heritage, but when one spends so much of one's time with another, and if that other is of tolerable empathy with a kind sense of humor, then often one ends up confiding information that one would not have otherwise. This is what eventually, a few murder stories in, happened between me and Gene. When I confided in him, I learned that he, too, was the disgraced offspring of a blue blood family. But while my family's assets were primarily invested in Virginia plantations, Eugene came from a different sort of money; his father owned Baughmann Industries and was the man who invested in Yuri Morislav, built their joint company, and thus founded Luxity. Though I thought I had left behind my high society values, this confession frankly made my jaw drop in a very unladylike way.

"Your father is Edward Baughmann? *The* Baughmann who funded *the* Yuri Morislav?" I choked out.

He nodded, and I could see that though he was estranged from them, he was still proud of his family.

"Oh yes. Morislav joined us for many suppers, mostly when I was young, of course. Quite an odd character — and busy now, naturally. Has a lot of inventing to do." The little quirk of his eyebrow gave lie to the nonchalant tone of voice. He was laughing at me inside.

"Well," I stammered. "Whatever happened to *you*?"

He stopped laughing inside.

"The usual. Differences of opinion, of philosophy. I thought the family company should go in a certain direction; my father disagreed. That was that." He shifted tack. "What about you?"

"The usual. Differences of opinion," I said.

And he was laughing again. That's how it was with Gene and me. In a way, we kept the social dance of our birth while managing the coarse, violent world that we had chosen for ourselves. Perhaps, though we had rejected our family's standings in favor of a tougher life, having someone to dance with gave the transition some grace, some fluency. It was a grace I needed while stepping through the early days of my job.

But then, somehow, someday, I was one of them. I laughed at a barber's joke without placing dainty fingers over my mouth. I wrote my notes in a quick, precise shorthand instead of asking interviewees to repeat their answers for the sake of my tidy penmanship. I came to love the romantic flickering of candles in the evening instead of the glare of expensive wave lights. I played a folk tune instead of Chopin on my piano-miniature. I even ate fried fish with my fingers, letting grease drip down my chin for just a moment before snagging it with my handkerchief. People on the street and at work called me "Ginnie" in friendly tones, and I woke smiling, eager for each day hunting my stories.

Other reporters talk about the first time the "Hunt" caught them, when they became true reporters instead of story-writers for a newspaper. For me, the Hunt began when I was seventeen.

But no, I'll save that for later.

The story I want to write now begins on a Monday at the *Journal*.

Prudence was there, and I was manning the tips desk. This was an ingenious idea of Mac's that he implemented when it became clear that most of the residents in our area had neither morsies nor telephones and couldn't send messages or calls to our tip receiver, but they could come in person, and come they did. The gossip in my old circles back in the Park neighborhood happened in curtained sitting rooms over tea and biscuits. The gossip here was spread in shops, on the street, at the flower stalls. It was mobile and changed by the hour. Tracking down a story took a very circuitous route, often without names, just "the butcher told me that..." and "well, according to the dressmaker..." Living on Starling and shopping in the area where I worked turned out to be not just the more affordable option for my tiny purse but also the most strategically intelligent decision of my career. I knew the "red-headed florist," the "brassy dame at the bakery," and even the "quiet, mousy boy" who ran in the gutters with his mongrel dog and belonged nowhere and to no one. All were vital in my line of work. And of course, there is always the fact that city people won't talk to folk from my old neighborhood, but they'll answer questions and gossip avidly with the dark-haired, hazel-eyed, quiet reporter who lives just around the corner on Starling.

I was speaking of the tips desk. That Monday, I was at the tips desk chatting with Prudence — or rather, she was chatting to me. She was my best friend, but conversations with Prudence ended up being rather one-sided. Not much of a talker myself (how Mother tried to break my tongue-tied habits with company!), our friendship flourished quickly. Besides Gene, she was my first friend at the *Journal*, and it was from her that I learned my way around not just the reporting business, but the living-in-the-city business.

While Prudence was talking, and I was rifling through the latest stack of tips for something that could make a second page story and not just a gossip column, a blonde woman in modest dress came through the door, which squeaked rudely on its hinges, matching the squeaks coming from the back hallway where Gene was working on his newest contraption away from the prying eyes of anyone who would report him to Mac. He didn't like the tips desk. The woman glided up to the desk, her hair swishing down her back in a way that suggested freedom, fluidity, and just a touch of sass. Even in the city, most women wore their hair up if not fashionably bobbed, but this woman's ringlets cascaded down her back like a golden waterfall. Admiration for her beauty filled me, leaving no room for disdain for her bold choice. She was stunning. Prudence immediately stopped mid-word and gave her full attention to the swaying locks. Prudence changed her hair every fortnight, using homemade dyes and even wigs. I could tell by her calculating look that she was scheming how to copy the curls and color with the bevy of hair tools in her apartment.

"Welcome to the *Franklin Journal*," I said. "Might you have some news for us?"

The woman stopped in front of the desk and stood uneasily, a hip cocked to one side. "It's... not exactly news." Her voice was hoarse but determined. "I want to put an ad in the *Journal*."

I tried not to show disappointment. The tips had been lean this week. I pushed aside the stack of papers I'd been perusing and pulled out a fresh scrap, unhooking my pen from my vest pocket.

"Of course. What would you like it to say?"

She looked around, then leaned forward, her slim hands resting on the top of the desk. "It should say, 'Wanted: the gentleman who calls himself Randall and wears the fern in his hat at the Orchid House. Milly needs to speak with you."

I stayed cool and wrote unhurriedly, but Prudence favored her with an open stare.

"The Orchid House? You a dancer there, Miss... Milly?"

The woman shook her hair back from her face and turned to smile at Prudence. "Sure am, love. I was out of commission for a few weeks after my baby was born, but I'm back now."

Prudence looked her up and down. "How long ago did you have the baby?"

Milly batted her eyelashes. "Four weeks ago."

Even I raised my eyebrows at this as I pushed her ad into the stack on the corner of the desk.

"That's never true," Prudence said, but her voice was shot through with admiration.

Milly shifted her hips. "I've got a living to make, haven't I? And I'm good at it, honey." She winked at Prudence, who moved forward and held out her hand.

"Prudence. Your name really is Milly?"

She shook her head as she gracefully took Prudence's hand. "No, it's my stage name. The Miltonia Orchid. My real name is Anne."

"So what's the story behind your ad, Anne?" The Hunt was in Prudence's eyes. She had a penchant for the dramatic gossip stories that never seemed to tickle my interest. I'd never met a middle-aged woman on the street who didn't read her column, though, which is why she hadn't been fired — yet. She was leaning in for the kill now, and I opened my mouth to advise her to let the woman go, but Anne's pretty hands clenched, and her eyes threw sparks.

"Here's how it is. This gent — Randall, he calls himself — came to my dances every other night for months. I knew he had a thing for me because he'd catch my eye after each dance, toss me an extra coin, call my name during the applause. Then he started seeing me after my shift. Pretty soon we were an item, and I was carrying his child. I named him Lawrence — a gentleman's son should have a gentleman's name, don't you think?" She stopped for breath and pushed her hair over her shoulder, where it fell in agitated waves. "Well. When I was about eight months along — couldn't hardly dance no more — he ups and disappears. Stops coming to the dances. Stops meeting me at our times. I thought he was going to give me a ring when the babe would be born — we were that close — but no. So I have Lawrence, and I'm wondering, what do I do with a gentleman's son with a gentleman's name and no father? That's when I decide. I'll find him myself. Get him to take us in. I've got Lawrence to think of now."

Her eyes dared Prudence to contradict her, but Prudence

was alight with interest. She'd nabbed a scrap of paper from my desk and was scribbling madly.

"What makes you think he's a gentleman?"

"His clothes, of course. And his speaking. Folks from the city don't talk like he does. And his hands. No manual labor there — he grew up soft." Her eyes twinkled mischievously. "No, mark me, he's from the Hill or one of them tree streets. He can afford a woman and a babe. To make it right."

Prudence stopped writing. "The dancer and the gent." Her face got that far-away look that always spelled trouble for whatever assignment Mac had given her. That story would be left in the gutter without so much as a by-your-leave.

Ironically, from upstairs, we heard a yell: "Prudence!"

In Prudence's hurried scrambling of paper, I heard a clamor of metal parts from the hallway. Gene would be cleaning up before Mac came down.

"Here," Prudence thrust a scrap into Anne's hands. "I'd love to meet up with you and, erm, discuss this further. I want to find him for you — in case the ad doesn't work. You can contact me there." She pointed to the address on the paper and fled through the hallway.

Anne seemed to take that as her cue to leave. The door squealed shut, and she made her way across the street as I watched through the big storefront window. The afternoon sunlight danced off her distinctive hair. A thought hit me.

"Oh no." I thumped down onto my chair in vexation.

"What?" Gene joined me and looked out the window to see why I was staring.

"I forgot to collect her fee for the ad." I sighed.

"How will the *Journal* drag on its existence now?" He leaned back in a chair, putting his arms behind his head.

"With less currency than it has, I suppose." I sighed again. I'd gotten no tips, fielded one unpaid ad, and while Prudence had another tawdry scandal to follow, I had nothing except a Mac-assigned story on the rising price of copper.

"Why the frown? The tips desk not living up to its promise?" Gene asked lazily, rolling a little metal gadget between his fingers.

I gave him a dry look. "What's that in your hand?"

He sat up and leaned forward to show me. "This genius invention is an electro-defense-ring. It deflects electrical attacks back onto the attacker." He slid it neatly on his finger and eyed it with affection.

"I see," I said. I didn't. Gene was always tinkering with some electro-weaponized-gizmo. Though he'd left his family behind, he couldn't seem to throw off their trade influence.

I looked at the clock that hung over the door. "It's almost time to meet the importer. Should we leave now?"

Gene turned his head to consider the clock as well. "A few extra minutes to walk there won't hurt. Let's go."

As we gathered our things, we heard stomping overhead.

"Wonder what ol' Mac is saying to Prudence this time," Gene muttered, shrugging on his coat. "Maybe he'll finally fire her."

"Don't say that," I begged.

"You should use your influence for good." He fixed me with a mock glare. "Tame your wild friend. If she showed up to work semi-consistently and actually hunted the stories he gave her, she'd be fine. Her tardiness could be forgiven, I'm sure."

I groaned quietly.

"You really should say something to her." He glanced over at me as we walked out the door to the sound of Mac's distant shouting.

"You think I haven't?" I shook my head. "This is Pru we're talking about, isn't it?"

"Ah well." He struck up a jaunty whistled tune. "Could be she'll mend her ways. It's always possible Mac could get through to her this time."

I adjusted my hat and rolled my eyes, not daring to hope

he was right. Shouting always slid right off Pru's back. I had the feeling her home with six siblings had been sonorous with raised voices. We ran across the street, dodging motor cars and bicyclists. No, I thought, it would come down to Mac deciding whether he liked the popularity of her stories enough to keep her. So far, she'd won out, but I always wondered what would cause him to change his mind.

When we'd finished our interview with the copper importer and headed our separate ways, my morsie printed me an answer from Pru.

<HE DID IT STOP COMING NOW STOP>

I groaned. I knew exactly what she meant.

When she arrived at my apartment later that night, I received the full story. Shortened, it ran like this:

Mac asked why she'd missed the deadline for the story he'd given her again. (This was the third time, I knew, though she deigned to leave that part out.) She told him she was working on a new story and his would have to wait. When she told him what it was, he'd blown up, talking about dragging his rich customers' names through the mud for a little excitement on her part. She'd replied crisply that that's what they deserved sometimes, and didn't most of his subscriptions come from downtown anyhow? When he'd argued, she'd lost her temper and asked if he was reluctant to print her story because he enjoyed the favors of dancers as well. That had been it for Mac. Her impudence today was a minor injury on a much larger bleeding wound.

"You're done!" he'd roared. "Get out! I'll replace you so quick you'll see stars!"

When she'd stayed a moment longer to protest, he'd actually pushed her through the door and slammed it, catching one of her feathers in the latch, which she'd had to pull free to replace in her hat.

Not surprisingly, she was completely recovered from the incident and was relishing the privilege of plunging me into all the details. One would think she was preparing her next column: "Vastly Popular Reporter Unjustly Fired from Long-Held Post."

"What are you going to do now?" I asked when she ran out of breath. Having made tea while she ranted, I handed her a cup and sat across from her at my little secondhand table.

Quite cheerful after her tirade, Prudence sipped her tea. "Oh, I'll find stories." She waved a hand dismissively. "I'll sell them to Mac. He'll take them. I can work on my own time now." Her eyes took on a manic glint. "Just think of the possibilities: without his hum-drum assignments, I'm free to hunt the stories I find! He'll see. They'll be more popular than ever, and then he'll beg to take me back and let me write whatever I want." She sat back with a self-satisfied thump, and the chair squealed ominously.

"Take care," I cautioned, reaching out, but she waved me away.

"I know. Weak back legs. I'm fine." She patted the chair familiarly. "Hasn't broken on me yet, has it?"

I considered her over my barely nibbled biscuit. Distress takes away my appetite. "Are you..." I colored slightly and swallowed. I still had difficulty speaking of vulgar topics. "Will you be able to..." I stammered to a halt. Prudence smiled tolerantly at me and lifted her cup from her saucer for a coy sip.

"Yes, dear Ginnie. I can afford my rent for this month. Not to worry." Her eyes widened, and she sat up, replacing the cup and saucer on the table. "Oh! I forgot. I can't stay any longer, though I'd love to chat more, but I just remembered I must do something with my hair tonight! It's gotten positively bedraggled. I can't interview that gorgeous dancer with a do like this." She patted her brunette faux bob and swept up her bag, heading for the door.

I rose and hurried after her. "Do you want to take a sandwich with you? Any biscuits?"

She laughed and patted my arm, already halfway out into the hall. "Sweet Ginnie. No, thank you. Ta-ta!"

And with that, she was gone.

I stood a moment longer, staring after her, still holding my biscuit.

It was probably silly of me to worry about someone who refused to have a care in the world, but I couldn't help thinking that one of those cares might eventually catch her, no matter her optimistic attitude, and then where would she be? No, I thought as I closed the door in her flippant wake, I'd keep worrying about her, even if the cares were a long time in coming.

2

The next day at the *Journal* — Tuesday, I believe it was — is foggy in my mind, and not just because the weather was dreadful. Prudence was often gone from the office, but simply the knowledge that she would not be coming in at all wilted my mood to match the sodden trees outside. As soon as we'd finished our last interview for the copper piece, I convinced Gene to stop by Prudence's apartment to check on her.

"I'm sure she's enjoying her freedom, Ginnie," he said, packing up the autophone (his invented recording device) and other equipment he'd used for the interview as thunder rumbled outside.

"I don't doubt that," I said, inspecting my umbrella. "I just want to ensure she's..." Ready for unemployment? I wasn't as positive as she was that Mac would take her stories freelance. Her parting words to him were good cause for a nice, long grudge.

Gene grabbed his own umbrella and shrugged. "Sure. Let's go."

When we got to Pru's apartment, I had to knock several times before I heard her muffled yell of "Come in!" I felt around her door frame for the key she kept hidden in a crack at the top and unlocked the door. Pru was always leaving her keys around where she couldn't find them and had finally settled on this emergency hiding place at my prodding.

We wiped our boots and navigated through the mess of scattered clothing, hats, shoes, curling irons, and crooked furniture that was her common living state and arrived in the kitchen where her head was upended in a bucket full of brown water.

"Whatcha doing, Pru?" asked Gene, poking his head into the kitchen and going wide-eyed at the sight. "You've got more to live for, doll, I promise. Don't do that."

Prudence made phony drowning noises.

"Stop it, Pru," I shivered. "She's just dying her hair, Gene." I took another look at the brown water. "For some reason, I thought you were going to try blonde this time."

She emerged, dripping and chagrined. "I was. I did. Last night, remember? But it didn't take." She held out a soaked strand and glared at it. "My brown was too dark, I think. I don't have enough powder to lighten it, so I decided to try red instead."

I picked up the little box of brownish powder and wiped the water droplets from its label. "Henna? This is what you're using now?"

"Ye-es," said Pru, now pouring water from a kettle over her head into the bucket. "Oww!"

"And now you're trying to burn yourself to death." Gene took the kettle from her and added cold water from the tap in her dish-filled sink. "Here."

Pru groped blindly for the kettle. Gene reached around a pile of food, took her hand and put it over the handle. As she poured the cooled water over her head, we watched the reddish stream join the darker brown in the bucket.

"Pru," I sighed, "why is all your food on the counter?"

"I'm letting it thaw," she answered, squeezing out her hair

venomously. "That ridiculous new-fangled machine froze it all again." I looked at the behemoth of a refrigerator to which she was pointing. Conceding her point, I pulled my watch from my pocket.

"You're meeting Milly tonight?"

"No, tomorrow. She's dancing too late tonight. She said tomorrow she's free after nine o'clock."

"Are you sure you want to do an interview alone at the Orchid that long after dark?" Gene was examining the moldy dishes with interest as he spoke. "Not that I frequent such places myself, but I've heard they get a bit rowdy after a dance."

Pru didn't answer. The bucket was overflowing, so she'd bumped him aside and was wringing out her hair over the dishes. I stayed silent. I'd never had much success talking to Pru about precautions when she was on a hunt. She'd braved much greater dangers for a story than staying out a little late. Her luck had been good so far. Plus, when she went out, she carried a sweet little blade in her bosom that had drawn blood more times than one would assume of a well-dressed woman like her. When I'd first arrived at the *Journal*, she'd insisted on teaching me a few lessons, and, after doing a few murder stories, I was happy to comply. My knife was in my boot.

"There," she said with satisfaction, and I saw that the water was now running clear. Gene handed her a dish towel and stepped back as she began the vigorous task of drying. When she'd finished drying her hair — and her upper body for good measure — she tossed the towel aside, barely missing Gene, who dodged just in time, and reached for the comb on the worktable.

"Why does she want to find this sheik so badly, anyway?" asked Gene, brushing off his suit.

"I think she wants him to marry her," Pru said with relish, yanking the last knots out of her hair. "She doesn't want to keep leaving her boy with her sick ma and dancing the night away. She wants to settle down."

"But with some society cake-eater? Isn't she aiming a bit high?"

"I don't think the money matters so much as the security. She knows he's got the money, he basically promised her he'd marry her before he disappeared, and now she has a baby to see to. She said she wants a better life for him." Pru shrugged and started pinning her hair up. "It makes for a great story."

"Maybe he died. Maybe that's why he's gone."

"I doubt it," Pru muttered through a mouthful of pins. "That's how men are, you know. Make promises, leave a girl hanging, go after a younger woman."

Gene looked offended.

"We'll leave you to your preparations then," I cut in quickly. "Please tell me if you need anything. Really, Pru."

She flashed me a grin and freed a hand to wave goodbye. "I'll see you Friday after I've found something. I did some digging on that Randall guy today, and I think I'm already onto something. Mac won't be able to say no!"

I signaled Gene, and we took our leave.

"You know," Gene said as he walked me home through the darkening streets. "If she's right about this cake-eater, he doesn't want to be found."

I nodded. "If he really is a gentleman, he won't marry her, will he?"

He shook his head. "Very unlikely. It could turn ugly instead. It would be better for the girl to find some other guy, someone her class. Settle down that way."

I sighed. "I saw her, Gene. She's not going to give up. If a girl like her gets an idea like that — especially with a baby to provide for — I don't think she'll stop."

"Well," he said. "Prudence shouldn't get involved. Let the girl get in trouble if she's determined to, but Pru doesn't have to get caught in it."

"You know her, Gene. She's more stubborn than anyone I've ever known. And if something happened to Milly, it would just make it a bigger story for her. She's a bloodhound with these hunts. She won't stop until she finds that man."

He kicked a stone across the street. "I guess we can't do anything about that. It's just her nature."

I rubbed my head and looked up at the apartment building. "Well, this is my stop. Thank you for seeing me home — and trying to talk her out of it. I don't think she hears a word I say most of the time."

He tipped his hat to me with a little bow. "At your service, as always. I'll see you tomorrow morning."

I smiled and waved as he turned to go, whistling carelessly.

My smile didn't last even to the end of the hallway. I couldn't get his words out of my head: *"It could turn ugly..."* He was right, I knew, and I didn't want Prudence in the middle of something like that. I knew the men in my father's circles, and I knew what could happen when a reputation was damaged. Shivering, I remembered my friend Nathaniel, and then forced the memory from my mind. The stakes for a gentleman keeping his reputation were much higher than for a working man like Mac or even Gene, now that he was fallen from high society like I.

That night I tossed and turned, my small bed creaking in protest. Finally, I got up to play my piano-miniature to calm my troubled mind. Tchaikovsky came to my fingers and did nothing to ease the worry that was steadily mounting. I gave up on the second movement and determined to go to Prudence's house after work and before her interview to convince her to leave the story alone. If I were truly her best friend, surely I could do that much. I went back to bed and gained a couple hours of rest before the sun peeked through my green curtains.

At work, the day dragged on as I struggled to transcribe our recorded interviews for my story.

"Gene," I said at one point, rubbing my face in exhaustion, "Why isn't Charlie's voice coming through on the audio? I know I recorded him."

Gene slid his chair over and smoothed his mustache thoughtfully.

"That was the one you did on your own?" He picked up the autophone and looked it over, then played it back. "When I was out sick?"

I nodded. "I was interviewing the economist, Williams, but his assistant, Charles, ended up giving the quote I wanted. The problem is that the only voices on this recording are mine and Williams'."

Around us the voices of other reporters rose and fell, and the sound of morsies lit up the general hubbub with sharp little dings. I massaged my aching head.

Gene stopped fiddling with the autophone and gave me a remonstrating look.

"Ginnie, did you program Charles' voice in?"

I groaned and lowered my head into my hands. "No."

Gene smacked his knee. "Well, that's your problem, doll. Sorry. Charles' voice isn't going to make its appearance on this recording." He patted the autophone fondly. "Not your fault, dear girl. I've told this careless reporter a million times that she's got to treat you right or you won't perform for her."

"But Gene," I pleaded, "They're gone! They sailed yesterday for Europe on a business trip!"

Gene shrugged. "Sorry, Gin. Not a thing you can do. If you don't press this button here," he leaned forward patronizingly to show me, but I pushed his hand away with another groan.

"I remember, I remember. It only records the voices I program in first. Why, Gene?" I smacked the desk in frustration.

He drew himself up and buttoned his coat in an aggrieved manner. "To cut out background noise, of course! How many times have I told you? It's the perfect solution for our noisy street recordings." He gestured to the air all around us. "You can hardly hear a thing in this din, and if we were recording with any old recorder, like those Bell devices, you'd barely make out a thing." He caressed the autophone and put it protectively in his breast pocket. "If you'd use it correctly, you'd thank me for the clear, perfect tone it creates."

I leaned back in my chair, holding my head and whimpering slightly.

He took pity on me. "Come on, Gin. You said you didn't get much out of that economist, anyway. Let's play back the other recordings — the ones *I* did —" he couldn't help but add, "and see if there's something you can work your writer magic on."

Somehow, I made it through the remaining hours until it was time to leave. As soon as the gigantic clock in the newsroom bonged, I was throwing on my coat and rushing out the door. Gene had left early to pick up a part for another gadget he was working on, so I didn't waste any time on goodbyes but headed straight to Pru's apartment.

When no one answered my knock, I deliberated for just a moment and then decided on a direct approach: I checked the door frame for the key, but my probing fingers found nothing. Feeling the agony of my day of waiting, I kicked the door and then tried the knob. It was unlocked.

"Thank heavens," I breathed. I walked through the apartment, calling for her, but soon realized she must have left already. "Probably getting dinner before the interview," I muttered to myself, admiring the newly mopped floor. Pru hardly ever cleaned, so it was a beatific sight when the impulse took her. A gentle lemon scent still lingered in the air — a vast improvement that almost covered the stale smell of unwashed laundry and burned food. I took a moment to send her a morsie, but despaired at her answering. When she was on the move, she hardly ever responded to messages. I liked to think of her as hyper-focused, though Gene may have used other terms. As I put away my morsie, I spotted her key lying on the table; I shook my head and made sure to lock the door as I left, wedging the key in the crack.

If I was going to find her before the interview, I needed to hurry. When checking all her favorite supper places yielded no results, I stopped at a diner to fill my own demanding stomach and to ponder what to do next.

By the time I'd finished my eggs and beans, I'd decided that the only sure way of finding Prudence was to go to the Orchid House, where she'd be meeting Milly after her dance. It was a little late at that point to convince her to forego the interview, but perhaps I could warn them both of the danger of continuing with the story. It was the only hope I had left, and I was exhausted. I gulped my cup of coffee, left an acceptable tip, and hurried out of the warm, smoky noise of the diner and onto the foggy, drippy streets.

Darkness was falling now, and I kept to the hazy glow of the streetlights, keeping my eyes open for any shady characters. I made it to the Orchid House with no scares and was debating whether to do the socially risky thing by going inside where it would be warm and light or stay outside where I had a better chance of catching Prudence before she found Milly. In the midst of my deliberation, I saw a golden-haired dancer make her way outside and peer around as if looking for someone.

"Milly!" I called, making my way around several Orchid patrons who were exiting the building. They looked at me in surprise, but moved on. Milly saw me and stopped.

"Where's Prudence?" she asked, still peering through the fog.

"I was hoping she'd be here already," I admitted, following her example. The night revealed no sign of a tardy Prudence, but suddenly it yielded something else: a wild, piercing scream that ended abruptly with an earsplitting CRACK. I jumped, and Milly gasped.

The patrons who had just left stopped in their tracks and turned to look down the alleyway that ran along the back of the Orchid House.

"Someone there?" they called out gruffly. We heard what sounded like running feet clattering through the alley to the other end — and then nothing. The men shrugged and moved on, but an evil premonition choked my throat.

"I'm going to investigate," I said, concentrating on keeping my voice from wavering. Milly nodded and clutched my arm for just a moment before moving ahead of me toward the alley. At the entrance, I bent down and took my knife from my boot as the premonition darkened my mind.

"Milly, wait," I hissed, and glanced up to see a man heading toward us from the street. "Sir!" I called out. "Sir! Would you step down this alley with us for a moment? We heard something..." I let out a breath of relief. It was a policeman, and I recognized him, though I couldn't remember his name. He hurried to my side.

"Miss, you shouldn't be out this late." He studied me with a friendly but confused look. "You're not a dancer, are you? Aren't you that press lady? What are you doing here in this weath—"

Another scream rang out.

"Milly!" I called and raced down the alley, the policeman following on my heels.

Milly's screams split the foggy air like a ship's whistle in menacing seas. Somehow, beyond the terrified part of my mind, I was relieved that the continued sound meant she was alive, but I also knew that one does not make such a sound unless something is very, very wrong.

3

Something was indeed very, very wrong. And this is where, for me, the nightmarish portion of my tale begins.

Milly's shrieks had turned into a whimpering wail, and she was crouching over what was unmistakably a dead woman.

My heart caught in my throat. "Is it...?" As I got closer, I saw that my fear was for naught.

It wasn't Prudence.

"Who is she, Milly?" I whispered, stooping down to hold her shoulders. A heavy putrid scent, like sulfur combined with charcoal and steak, assaulted my nose, and I gagged.

"It... it's Ludisia," she gasped. "Her... her dress..."

I covered my nose and mouth and bent down to look more closely at the corpse, immediately realizing why she mentioned Ludisia's dress. It would be impossible to identify her another way. Her face looked as if it had been blasted into the back of her skull. Singed hair ringed what had been her head and trailed black lines to her chest where her distinct, low-cut dress revealed a tattoo of an orchid on her left breast.

The policeman was tapping rapidly into his morsie. "Excuse me, ladies," he said firmly. "You're going to need to step back now. I'll take care of this." He stowed his morsie in his pocket and held out his hands. "Come on now, up you get. This is no sight for a dame."

Milly was still weeping, but she let me pull her away. I took the hand offered me and stood, bringing her with me.

Shock was encasing my mind, but deep inside, another voice took over.

You have a job to do, it urged.

I pushed aside the walls of icy terror and embraced my choice of action.

"We'll be over here," I told the policeman. I took a steadying breath, drew Milly aside, and retrieved the pad of paper and pen I always kept in my vest.

"Milly, Ludisia is gone. I'm dreadfully sorry. You know what we need to do now, don't you?" I lowered my head to look her in the eye as she raised her face from her hands. "We need to give the police all the information that we have so they can catch her killer. Do you understand?"

Though her red, dilated eyes were still staring in horror, she turned to me and nodded.

"Tell me now," I said, pushing my hair back and shaking my pen. "Who was she and when did you see her last?"

When the policeman joined us after examining the body, I could give him concise answers to the questions I'd known he would ask while Milly slowly sagged against me. He asked us for our addresses when I was done and then stowed away his own pad of paper.

"The detective will be here any minute now," he told us. "Why don't you sit here on these steps while we wait?"

"Wait for what?" A brusque, authoritative voice rang out through the fog as we sank down.

The policeman jumped and clutched his hat. "Gave me a fright there, sir. Waiting for you. These young ladies," he gestured to us, "were in front of the Orchid House when it happened. They heard her scream."

"Well then," the voice said, "let's get to work."

When I stood and he stepped into the light of the lamppost at my back, I saw that the detective was tall — too tall — and though deep lines ran across his forehead, the rest of his face was young, and his eyes were disconcerting. One had the idea that he saw much more than what one tried to present to the world.

"That's you, Pritchard, isn't it?" he barked. "You got their statements?"

The policeman was standing at attention. "Yes sir! Here they are, sir. The coroner is on his way, sir."

"Very good. Get to work roping off this scene. We don't want visitors mucking about. Wait here, please, ladies."

He followed Pritchard's path carefully, sweeping his light from side to side, and then he squatted to examine the body. We waited for what seemed forever, and I eventually sat back down with Milly, rubbing my eyes and squinting down the alley to study his progress.

Finally, just when I thought he'd perhaps forgotten about us, he returned. He was shuffling through Officer Pritchard's pad of paper, frowning and licking his finger to turn the pages. After scanning the notes, he glanced up and caught my eye.

"Are you Miss Harper or Miss Smith?" he asked, removing his hat and using it to gesture at me.

"Miss Harper. This is Miss Smith." I moved aside so he could see Milly. She was curled up on the steps, smoking. She gave him a small wave with her cigarette when his eyes shifted to her. "And what do we call you?" I asked.

"Detective Ward will do. Miss Smith, you are the one who found the deceased, correct?"

A low rumble of thunder sounded as Milly pushed herself back to her feet and nodded.

"We worked together, her and me," she said. "She was a good dancer."

The Orchid House began spewing patrons out its front doors. I held my wrist up to the light and squinted at my watch: it was only nine thirty. It seemed like an eternity since we'd found Ludisia's body.

Detective Ward was scanning the notes again. "I see Pritchard got your information. I will send you a morse if I need to speak with you further. What are you doing, Miss Harper?"

"I'm sending for my assistant," I told him as I transmitted a message to Gene, having just realized that he would berate me endlessly tomorrow if I didn't call him in. "I'm a reporter for the *Franklin Journal*. We'll want to cover this story." I shot Milly a glance, regretting my callousness in the face of her grief. Detective Ward followed my eyes.

"Would you like an escort home, Miss Smith?"

Milly shook her head and bent down to extinguish her cigarette on the steps. "I'm hoping to go now, though, sir," she said, and he nodded, tipping his hat to her.

"You can find me at the precinct if you think of anything else that could be helpful," he said.

As she disappeared into the mist, he turned back to me with a furrowed brow. "And what was a reporter for the *Journal* doing here at nine o'clock in the evening with a dancer from the Orchid House?"

I stowed my morsie in my pocket. "Trying to find my friend, actually."

"Another dancer?" he asked. I searched him over for a moment, trying to ascertain if his voice held disdain, but his eyes were stern, not derisive, and I decided his was an honest question.

"No, another reporter," I answered. "She was supposed to meet Miss Smith here about a story. But she hasn't come." Speaking these words brought back all the tension and worry I'd felt over Pru all day — and it had been a very long day. I rubbed my head.

"Does she often miss her appointments?" he asked, now tapping notes into what looked like a large morsie.

"Yes," I admitted, checking my watch again. "Yes, she does. But I'm concerned about this story she's following, so I was trying to track her down before they met." I looked out into the mist. "I suppose that's unnecessary now."

Detective Ward looked up. "Yes, I would assume so."

"Ginnie? Ginnie!"

I turned to the street and spotted Gene jogging toward us through the gloom.

"Here," I called, waving.

"What on earth are you doing here? Hello, Officer," he said, doffing his cap and raising his coat collar. "Brr. Do you realize what time it is?"

"Gene, a dancer was killed a little while ago," I said, taking out my notes. "I was hoping you would get a statement from Detective Ward on autophone for our story tomorrow."

"Of course, of course," Gene said, pulling it out. "But that doesn't explain what *you* were doing here when a murder happened."

"I was trying to find Pru," I snapped. "But I found a body instead. Will that do for you?"

"Sorry," he said, stepping back a little. "So, Officer, do you have a statement for tomorrow's *Journal*?"

The detective had been watching us with narrowed eyes and tapping on his morsie at the same time. At Gene's words, he sighed a little and stopped. Behind us, Officer Pritchard was talking to more policemen who had arrived. I concentrated on taking more notes while Detective Ward gave Gene a terse statement of the case, informing the public that Precinct Eight was doing everything they could to apprehend the murderer.

"I wonder if they investigate slightly less, given the victim's profession," Gene muttered as he wrapped the autophone and slipped it into his pocket.

"Of course not." Detective Ward was apparently blessed with excellent hearing. "The victim was a person. Her profession dictates nothing about the case, except perhaps giving clues as to the location of the murderer and potential enemies."

"Well, good," Gene said, snapping a photo of him. "Personally, these clues give me nothing but the creeps," he whispered to me as he headed toward the murder scene for more pictures.

"Are you done here?" asked the detective, still frowning.

"I think so… oh wait, no. Do you have any idea what kind of weapon could have done that?" I gestured toward the corpse. The street was beginning to blur in my vision; I wasn't sure if the strange effect was because of the horrid weather or the exhaustion that was slowly overcoming most of my senses.

"I can't give a statement on that currently," he said.

Which meant he didn't know, I translated. I had a source over at a munitions factory: I'd call them in the morning. As I rubbed my head again, I tried to think of anything I was missing. "I did spell the names of your colleagues correctly, didn't I?" I handed him my paper and resisted the urge to sit on the steps, instead checking my watch again. Ten o'clock. I thought longingly of my lumpy mattress and feather pillow. Detective Ward handed the paper back with a nod of affirmation. "Gene?" I called hesitatingly. He appeared out of the alley, waving farewell to the policemen at the scene.

"Ready." He gave me a thumbs up. "I'll walk you home, Gin."

He took my arm and nodded to Detective Ward, who said shortly, "Make it quick. The young lady is about to fall asleep standing up." He looked me over and said gruffly, "I'll be watching the *Journal*'s front page. Quote me right, Miss Harper."

"I will," I promised huskily as Gene led me away through the eerie streets.

I hardly heard his lecture on the walk home, and all I

remember after that is collapsing into my bed, forgetting to even close the curtains before submitting to unconsciousness.

I do remember waking sometime in the night, heart racing, covering my mouth to hold back a scream from a vivid nightmare I'd just experienced where the body in the alley had been Pru instead, eyes open and empty, a hole blasted through her chest… and then every step I took brought me to a new body: Gene, Mac, my father, Nathaniel…

Biting my lips till they bled, I scrambled for my morsie and sent a message to Pru, then finally fell back into a fitful sleep, waiting for a message that didn't come.

4

I was only halfway present at my work the next day. My source at the munitions factory had never heard of a weapon that did the sort of damage I had seen the previous night, so I was no closer than Detective Ward to finding out what the murder weapon had been. My source did mention the Vangees company if I wanted to investigate further, so I jotted the name down for later and worked on my draft of the murder story.

By the afternoon, Gene had to repeat himself multiple times to tell me that Mac wanted to see me in his office about our assignment. I slapped my cheeks, ripped the story off my typewriter, and hustled up the stairs.

"You wanted to see me?" I asked, stepping through his doorway. Mac slapped down the paper he was reading and gestured me forward.

"Yes, yes. What's your status on the murder story?"

I stifled a yawn and blinked hot, dry eyes. "Here's the first draft." I handed it to him.

Scanning it quickly, Mac nodded his approval.

"Is that all, sir?" I asked, shifting my feet.

"One more thing." Mac picked up a cigar and lit it. "Is the partnership with Gene working out?"

I was taken aback. "Yes, sir." Just as it has for the past five years, I thought to myself impatiently.

"You're wondering why I ask."

I nodded, stifling another yawn and clasping my hands behind my back.

He tapped the paper on his desk. It was the *Blue Rose*, the high society paper from Oak Hill, or the Hill, as it was normally called. I knew Mac read his competitor's papers to see if there was anything we missed, but I didn't understand why he was pointing to a small article on the fourth page until I leaned in closer and saw the name Eugene. I reached for the paper, and Mac pushed it toward me. "You didn't know?"

I shook my head slowly, scanning the little column that announced the engagement of Eugene Baughmann to a Miss Helen Derwitz.

"She's the daughter of Chester Derwitz on the Hill, isn't she?" Mac stabbed the paper with his cigar and almost lit it on fire. "That energy mogul who put up the static balloons?"

I nodded slowly. I even knew Helen, though her family lived on the Hill and mine was from the Park. They rubbed shoulders with Gene's family because of the close tie with Morislav's business. Mr. Derwitz created the balloons that kept the electricity running through our city and collected the energy fee from its citizens for their use. Gene's estranged family worked closely with the energy keepers in developing their new products. He must have met her through that professional relationship, though I was frankly astonished that his black sheep status hadn't upended the match.

"Surprised?" Mac grunted.

I didn't answer immediately. Replacing the paper gently on his desk, I forced a smile. "We owe him congratulations, clearly. Perhaps a small celebration here at the *Journal* before he leaves?"

"So you think he'll leave, too." Mac scowled.

I shrugged, still smiling, but I knew. No Hill family would have a son-in-law who worked at a downtown newspaper for a living — especially as a low-paid recording assistant to a female reporter. Gene would have other plans.

"We'll miss him," I said.

Mac grunted again. "We'll miss his gadgets! That autophone has been a lifesaver. Get him to leave it with us, will you? Or two or three for good measure." He paused a moment, eyebrows drawn in a severe V-shape. Then he frowned at me. "You're dismissed. Scram. Finish up that murder story before he leaves."

"Thank you, sir." I closed the door gently behind me and walked downstairs, a headache starting. The sound of typewriters and morsies rang all around me as I descended to the newsroom.

"Ready to play back the interviews?" Gene asked, looking up from my desk as I approached. I'd tracked down a few of the dancers at the Orchid House that morning to find out more about Ludisia for our story. With Gene interviewing the police at the precinct, I'd ordered myself to remember the program button on the autophone so I wouldn't embarrass myself again. The result was a nice selection of interviews with dancers and statements from the policemen.

"Yes."

He vacated my chair, and I sank into it as he pulled up a wooden one for his own use.

"What's wrong, Gin?" he asked, pushing papers aside and pulling out the autophones. "You look tired today."

I pasted on a smile. "I'm fine. It appears that you deserve my congratulations, Gene. We'll miss you, but I'm very happy for you."

He looked startled. "Wha —... oh! You heard about me and Helen, then?" He scratched his head sheepishly. "Sorry I hadn't told you yet. I haven't dared to believe that she'd see it through. Her family's awfully wealthy — you know."

I nodded. "I remember Helen. She's a sweet girl."

He shifted in his seat. "Yeah, yeah she is. Say, Ginnie, you really look beat. What's wrong?"

Despite my best intentions to the contrary, my eyes filled, and I fished in my pocket for my handkerchief. "I... I'm worried about Pru... and you were one of my first friends here, and…" I sniffed. "I suppose… I'm sad you'll be leaving us."

Gene looked wretched as he handed me his own handkerchief. "Ah Gin, I'm sorry I didn't tell you. Did Mac?" When I nodded, he grimaced, putting a hand over his face. "What a rotten way to spread the news. I didn't want to get my hopes up and have you sad about losing a partner, so I waited too long. Forgive me?"

"There's nothing to forgive," I protested, blowing my nose squeakily. "I really am happy for you. You'll have more... resources for your inventions now, won't you?"

Despite his efforts to appear unassuming, he positively glowed. Even with the anxiety battering my mind, I couldn't help but be glad for him. "Yes, yes, getting back on the Hill gives me an advantage in that area. I don't have to have my parents' approval anymore. I can develop the products I want and patent them without going through my father. Helen is very supportive; I think we'll get along real well."

I smiled at him. "That's wonderful. Really, Gene, I mean it. I wish you all the best."

Gene smiled back and affectionately smacked my shoulder with the sodden handkerchief I handed him. "Well, I'm not leaving before this thing gets written, so let's get back to it, shall we?"

I nodded and tried to banish my worries as we tackled tomorrow's story.

For the third day in a row, I found myself hurrying along

the street after work to Prudence's apartment. When my messages had gone without reply, I'd decided to try there again, as I couldn't shake the horrible feeling that something had happened to her as well. It was probably the ghastly things I'd seen the night before mingled with the terror of the nightmares my mind had conjured, but at times, one simply cannot remove a feeling of dread without learning the truth — no matter what form the truth takes. I hoped today it would take the form of relief; I hoped Pru would be home.

She was not.

There were still dishes rotting in the sink, still the smell of spoiled milk and burned food now that the lemon scent had worn off, and her hats and shoes were still everywhere.

I stood in the middle of the living room and fought the fears that threatened to collapse me.

"She's fine," I whispered fiercely, swiping at the tears that escaped from my eyes. "She's just on the Hunt. How many times have I called her erratic and nomadic when she gets the scent of a dramatic story?"

I let my mind wander for just a moment before making a decision. I'd go back to the Orchid House and ask Milly if Pru had caught up with her today.

When I arrived there, though, Milly was nowhere to be found.

"She's the one found Luddy the other night, yeah?" drawled a redhead lounging in front of her makeup station with a cigarette. "Figured she was too worked up to come into work today. She and Luddy were close. Came over together from the Rose Palace a few months ago." She took a long drag and saw my blank face. "You know, the dance house closer to the Hill? On the other side of town? Yeah, I guess you wouldn't get over there. They came here a' cause Luddy was gettin' hounded by some gent from the Hill. Needed a new location. Fresh start."

"Did you tell the detective about the gentleman?" I asked, taking notes. "He'd want to know about him."

"Yeah, probably. Can't remember. The tall sheik? With all the questions?"

I nodded.

She took another long drag. "Yeah, someone would've mentioned him. He was a piece of work from what Milly said. Why you lookin' for Milly, anyway? Weren't you here earlier today?"

"I'm not here for the case," I said quickly, moving out of the way of a crowd of dancers heading for the stage. "I'm looking for a friend." I stopped. "You wouldn't have seen her, would you? Her name is Prudence — she may have come looking for Milly, too?"

The redhead screwed up her face in concentration. "Nah, nah, don't think so. Sorry."

I tried not to look disappointed. "Don't be sorry. Thanks for your help. Oh, do you happen to know where Milly lives?"

"I'm full of disappointment for you today," she said, eyeing me regretfully as another dancer called her onto the set. "I don't." She got up from her seat and shook her head. "Lotsa girls aren't showing up to work today. Probably nervous about the killing."

"Well, thanks anyway," I said and turned to go.

"Bye!" she called after me. "Tell that sweet-looking detective hi from Cat if you see him, will you?"

I waved and made my way through hurrying dancers back out to the street. Stopping on the steps where I'd sat last night, I thought for a moment, then sent a message to the detective asking where Milly lived. I waited several minutes on the steps, pondering and watching the evening passersby as the sun slowly sank, emitting an orange glow striped across the sky. Little pops accented the evening, a common background noise of Luxity that I didn't normally notice.

How many of these people hurrying by knew a woman's

life had been snuffed out just a few yards from where they were walking now? Were any of them acquaintances of the murderer? Perhaps they sat with a cold-blooded killer at supper or laughed with him — or her — in the evening before a cozy fire. Or was one of these innocent-looking wanderers the person who had blasted a woman out of life — just over there, in the darkening alley behind me?

I shivered and stopped thinking. Shifting my attention elsewhere, I saw that the sun was almost halfway below the horizon, but after checking my morsie to confirm that I hadn't gotten a message from Detective Ward or Pru, I decided rather recklessly to go to the Rose Palace to check for Milly there. If I didn't find her, then at least one of her old friends should know where she lived. Somehow I would catch up to her and Prudence — and with any luck at all, it would be tonight.

5

Not surprisingly, luck was something I would not experience for quite some time, and I certainly did not enjoy its benevolence that night. First of all, I made three wrong turns trying to find the Rose Palace, and one stop for directions led me to a rather rude man who made some quite shocking insinuations before I slapped him and hurried off. Finally, I found the Rose Palace, lit from behind by the last vestiges of sunset, but no luck met me there either. Instead, tragedy reared its hideous head.

This time, I knew the victim. This time, it was Milly's murder scene I found.

Anne. I should say Anne, seeing as that was her given name, and in death one ought to be remembered for who one is, not what one does for cold currency.

Anne was dead, already surrounded by policemen. Her body had been found by a drunk patron behind the Rose Palace in a back alley. Her face, too, had been blasted into anonymity, but the long, luscious blonde hair and tattooed orchid on her breast had been recognizable enough to identify her even before the coroner took over.

"She has a rose tattoo on her thigh," a policeman was

telling Detective Ward as I blinked back tears and slipped through the throng of people gathered outside the alleyway.

"Just as the coroner's report said of the first victim," Ward replied, frowning heavily and tapping into his oversized device.

"They danced together here," I cut in, breathless from the push through the crowd.

Detective Ward saw me and tipped his hat in greeting, frowning even harder. "Yes, yes, we know that. They have the tattoos designating their place of employment. But what are you doing here, Miss Harper? I find your appearance on murder scenes uncanny."

"It's a bit of a coincidence, I'm afraid," I said, and my voice caught a bit as I saw Milly's body behind him. "I'm looking for my friend still and hoped Milly could tell me where she was… and that someone at the Rose Palace could tell me where Milly lived…" I trailed off, looking up at the dance hall's neon lights and thinking of last night, when Milly and I had found Ludisia dead. Now I was here, and her body was lying just beyond the line of policemen restraining the curious crowd. Detective Ward brought me back to the present.

"I don't believe in coincidences," he said. "Why don't you come with us and get the information for your paper, and then we'll talk."

At his gesture, the officer in front of me moved aside, and I followed him to the scene of the murder where I interviewed him with the autophone, making sure to use the program button first for my voice and his.

"She was found at seven fifteen in the alleyway behind the Rose Palace," Detective Ward said into the 'phone. "It looks as though she was killed in the same way as the victim last night, though we do not have a time of death yet. We know that both murder victims were dancers, first for the Rose Palace and then more recently for the Orchid House. The police are working very hard to ensure that their murderer — or murderers — are found and with no further loss of life."

"Do you expect more murders?" I asked quietly into the 'phone, then held it out to him again.

"The evidence for that is inconclusive. I would suggest not. These two murders may be linked, as the victims were friends and colleagues, suggesting a limited scope of victims, so there is no reason to predict more."

"And what evidence have you found of the murderer? Anything that would give you reason to take anyone into custody?"

"That is confidential."

When I raised my eyebrows at him, he gestured to me to switch off the autophone.

"I will tell you, Miss Harper, that no, we have not — not yet. But I will also tell you not to include that in your article. The public rarely understands our process, and we don't need angry folk battering at our doors demanding suspects."

"You don't trust people with the truth, then?"

"No," he said flatly. "Usually, no." He studied my face as I stowed the autophone. "You are thinking something mutinous, Miss Harper."

I fumbled the autophone and looked up, blushing. "Not mutinous, sir. I am simply in disagreement."

"You think that the average person can handle the facts of what we do?" He shook his head. "I find you quite optimistic, Miss Harper."

"On the contrary," I replied, squaring my shoulders. "I disagree with the philosophy of what you have said. What they do with it is not as important as the fact that they are given it. Individual responsibility is the individual's, not mine. My job is to provide them with the truth, no matter what they decide to do with it." I studied his face. "And you find me silly now."

I couldn't discern what thoughts were hidden behind his

piercing eyes. "No, not silly, Miss Harper. Misguided perhaps."

"Trust me in this," I said. "I was misguided in much. This, however, I have learned myself, needing no guidance except that of experience."

"And experience tells *me* otherwise," he said sardonically. "My experience leads me to keep as much as possible from the irresponsible public."

"And my experience tells me that nothing is more important than that the public, which at times has the power of life and death, knows the truth before the lie ruins lives."

We studied each other for a moment. Unbroken by our silence, the electric hum of the city continued around us. Our mutual gaze was broken when an older officer with a limp crossed the path between us.

"They're ready to move the body, sir," he said in a strong northern accent. "Miss," he added, tipping his hat to me.

"Right," Ward said, pulling his eyes away from mine. "Is the coroner here?"

"No, sir, but the wagon is."

"Wait here, if you would, Miss Harper," Ward said, walking with the officer.

It was difficult to watch them raise Anne's body and place it in the wagon, but I felt that I owed her a kind of farewell. I thought of her mother and baby and wondered if they had been told the news yet. The ache in my chest pounded in concert with the rising and falling voices of the crowd, most of whom were strolling away now. I remembered another crowd, seven years ago, watching curiously as Nathaniel's body was loaded onto a wagon to be taken away. The vision was blurry in my memory as I had been crying too heavily to see anything clearly. Time passed oddly in the months after his death; I remember the disbelief when I found that his father had bribed his way out of a prison sentence after what he'd done… simply because Nathaniel told him he was leaving the lucrative family business to become an artist instead. Everyone believed the newspaper story as well: that Nathaniel had committed suicide upon receiving a fatal diagnosis of an agonizing disease. He'd taken the courageous way out — on his own terms. His family was devastated, but also proud in a way. When I read those words in crisp black-and-white in my father's newspaper, I vomited — not once, but many times over the next month as people went about their everyday lives in ignorance and as Nathaniel's family unraveled. I had seen what happened: I had been there, feeling admiration and awe for my best friend when he announced his intentions to leave high society.

I knew the truth.

So did Nathaniel's mother. She had killed herself not long after.

Because of my father's reliance on Nathaniel's family for trade and social reasons, I had been hushed. The truth had been buried. In my confusion and despair, I had put up no fight but let myself be silenced.

As I saw it happen again in my memory, my stomach rolled in response. Not here, I commanded my body.

Staring up at a streetlight, I forced my lungs to take in several deep breaths, letting the humid air whoosh slowly back out of my mouth and into the darkening street. I clenched and unclenched the autophone in my pocket.

The truth must always be known, Detective Ward, I thought. Someday, perhaps, you will understand.

But right now I had a job to do — the job I had chosen in order to make up for my past, the job I had used to follow in Nathaniel's footsteps, to honor him by leaving a life of lies and pursuing a life of displaying the truth, a life that did not befit a young lady of my status, as my parents had shouted. I took the shouts, absorbed them, seeing again what Nathaniel's father had done. In a way, on that day five years ago when I declared my independence, I had almost hoped that Nathaniel's fate would also be mine: that my responsibility would be over, that I wouldn't have to face a new life on my own, that penance for my silence would finally be paid.

You see, I am not as courageous as my friend was.

When I was left with mere banishment, I knew that the only thing to do was to earn my way into the job that I'd decided on as soon as my fog of mourning had lifted and my years of life stretched out in empty, ugly pettiness before me: I would be a reporter. I would investigate and publish the truth for all to see, day in and day out. For over a year, I had planned, practiced, written. And upon my exit, I was ready.

Now, my job was to follow this case, to tell the citizens of Luxity what someone had done to two of its women, to urge them to cooperate with the police in their efforts for justice.

So I waited for Detective Ward, and I scribbled notes for my story that would be read all over the city tomorrow.

6

"Tell me about this friend you're trying to find," Detective Ward said, joining me under the lamppost. All the other bystanders had left, and only a few policemen remained. Ward rubbed his head and replaced his hat.

"Well," I said, trying to decide what to tell him. "You may have seen her column in the *Journal*. Her name is Prudence Bailey."

When he shook his head, I elaborated. "She writes… well, gossip columns, I suppose."

A look of comprehension crossed his face.

"She was fired, actually, this week, but she's convinced that she'll get hired back on as a freelance writer because people love her columns."

"She was following a story with the victim tonight, correct?" he asked, tapping determinedly into his oversized morsie.

"Yes. I'm not sure if they met since I saw her last, but—"

"Which was…?" He paused and waited.

"Tuesday," I said promptly. "I saw her Tuesday. They were supposed to meet yesterday, but I don't think they did unless it was very late."

"So it's been two days since you saw or heard from her, and she's often out of touch."

I nodded. "It's probably silly of me to worry, since it is very typical of her, but with all this…" I gestured to the alley, wanting him to understand.

"It's an atypical situation." He nodded, then glanced at his watch. "Do you have time to go to her house?"

"Tonight?"

He nodded again.

"Yes." I didn't hesitate, thinking of how badly I'd slept since I'd seen her last.

"You can lead me there?" he asked.

"Yes," I said. "Are we able to go now?"

He gallantly indicated the street with his arm. "By all means."

We walked quickly. Night had fallen, and the lampposts were the only source of light as the overcast sky veiled the moon and stars.

I remembered walking to her house with Gene on Tuesday, worried about Pru being fired. Now I was hurrying through the dark streets with a detective, and my worries were much more serious. How much can change in only two days! I sighed a little to myself, and despite the clopping of hooves and the splashing of wagon wheels in puddles, Ward heard me and glanced over.

"Are you well, Miss Harper?"

Remembering how I'd just lectured him on the importance of truth-telling, I decided on honesty.

"No, sir."

A stiff wind ruffled my hair, tugging at our hats, and I grimaced, pulling my coat more tightly around myself.

Ward secured his hat and offered his arm.

"It's chilly tonight," he said as a spatter of rain struck our faces.

I nodded and took his arm. It was warm and firm, and I

felt my muscles relax slightly. It was helpful to lean on someone: the streets were darker than I liked, especially with the wet cobblestone to traverse. My feet had been slowly, painfully protesting over the last mile to Pru's apartment.

The dark and cold added to my overburdened mind, and I found myself blurting out my worst fear as a question.

"Have you ever lost a friend, Detective? A… a good friend?" The inkiness of the night hid my blush. My mother would faint, seeing me on the arm of a common detective and hearing me — horror of horrors — asking him a personal question! But I did not have the luxury of a friend nearby, and the anxiety that was creating a great, aching stone in my stomach needed an outlet, a conversation — no matter who happened to be the confidant.

Detective Ward considered me for a moment, and again I could not tell what he was thinking. Many people reveal their thoughts through their eyes, the windows of the soul, as some say, but Ward's windows always seemed to be shuttered. Their piercing quality did not abash me now, in my desperate state. Instead, I stared at them, waiting for his answer.

"I don't know what to make of you," he said. "You were born into a family in the Park, weren't you?"

I was taken aback. "Yes, but… how ever did you know?" My mind was filtering back through our conversations, trying to remember if I had said anything that would reveal my heritage. I could think of nothing.

He looked down the street. "You are not used to people knowing?"

I shook my head. "I don't tell anyone."

He raised his eyebrows, then nodded in understanding. "Ah. Yes. You talk to people for a living — there are many who would refuse an interview with a Park woman. But I wouldn't be surprised if more people know than you realize — not perhaps the Park specifically, but it isn't difficult to miss your… gentle upbringing."

I was offended. "I think my store-bought dress disguises that quite well."

Was that a minuscule smile I saw pulling at his stern mouth?

"Perhaps. For some." He glanced at me out of the corner of his eye. "I was engaged to a woman of your former status once. That may have helped my deduction."

"Was she from the Park as well?"

"No," he said slowly. "No, she is not from here."

Some insanity drove me on.

"What happened to her? You did not marry?"

"She and I did not marry, no. She married one from her own class instead. I was… away."

I did some deduction of my own.

"In the war?"

He looked down at me and nodded.

"I'm sorry," I said, feeling foolish.

I heard the ding of my morsie and was about to pull it out when he spoke again. There was a hard look in his not-as-shuttered eyes this time.

"You asked me a question before. When I tell you I was part of a division that saw a significant amount of action, then I am sure you can discern the answer for yourself."

What can one say to such a statement? Suddenly, watching Nathaniel die did not seem an event that set me apart as unique in this world. How many friends had he seen killed in a foreign land with no comfort of home to soothe the pain? I shuddered; I had no words to begin the conversation again. Instead, I retrieved my morsie from my coat pocket, ripped off the little slip of paper it had printed, and stopped dead.

It was a message from Prudence.

The message read, <SORRY STOP BEEN POKING AROUND STOP FOUND ANOTHER STORY STOP HOW ARE YOU STOP CANT WAIT TO SHOW MAC WHAT I GOT STOP>

I felt like laughing hysterically and instead let out a small hiccough.

"It's her," I said. "She's fine."

"Is she home?" he asked.

I was already tapping back. "I'll find out."

We huddled under a street lamp while we waited for an answer. It came back within a minute.

<NO STOP ON A HUNT STOP SEE YOU NEXT WEEK STOP>

"Oh," I said, a little disappointed. "No, she's still investigating. She said she'll see me next week, so it must be an involved story. She only takes that long if she's found something… excessive." I smiled at him. The relief I felt was so overwhelming I lost track of where I was stepping and stumbled.

Ward grasped my arm and settled me gently on my feet until I was sturdy once more.

"Very good, Miss Harper," he said. "May I have her code so I can contact her? You said she was on a different story now?"

I nodded. "I wonder if she ever saw Milly after that first day at the office. She probably knows nothing about what happened to her if she's been investigating all this time. She must have gotten sidetracked right before they were to meet." A long sigh exited my chest as I wrote out her morsie code for him. "I can't tell you how relieved I am. Why, I may even be able to sleep tonight." I tore the paper off and handed it to him.

He tucked it into his coat pocket. "Yes, sleep. That's a good idea. Come, Miss Harper. Will you allow me to walk you home?"

I took his arm again, happily ignoring the aches in my feet and head. "It cannot be right for me to feel this much relief when a woman has just been killed."

"You are overtired, Miss Harper," he said. "You may feel as you like. Sleep will help."

"Yes," I said, my mind suddenly running through the notes I had taken for tomorrow's paper. "Yes, I think you're right. I live this way, Detective."

We parted at my door; he lifted his hat and bowed me in, and I gave him a small curtsy, something I hadn't done in quite some time.

Once I undressed and lay on my lumpy mattress, sleep was more elusive than I'd hoped it would be. Perhaps I was simply overtired, as Ward had said. I have found that sleep is a nagging tease when I've gone too long without a proper taste of it. That night it danced just out of my reach, taunting me with grisly images of dead women and baiting me with different wordings for my story. Perhaps I should begin it a different way, with more of a shocking angle, or in somber respect of the victims, or...

However, finally, I caught up to my mocker, banished the

distractions that it held, and floated away on its dreamy wings. Whether my mind knew I was too unwell for nightmares or because of something else, I experienced no dreams that night, and the next morning was the most normal morning I'd had in a week. The office was its usual chattery, pinging bustle, and Gene was relaxed and jovial as always, though the bags under his eyes matched my own. It had been an eventful week for our little team, cobbling these stories together. He was glad to hear about Prudence, though he wasn't as surprised as I was that she'd found another story to hunt; he goaded me for worrying as much as I had. We transcribed my notes from the previous night together, and he happily told me about his plans after his marriage to Helen. His jaunty jabber made me smile and helped take my mind off the murders we were describing to the public.

Yes, evil people existed in the world, I thought, people who would murder and hate and hide, but there were always good people, too, and marriage ceremonies and other cheerful occasions.

"I don't suppose I'll garner an invitation to the wedding," I quipped with an ironic grin. "Now that you're moving back into society, you can't bring your black sheep friends with you."

"Ah, sure I can," he chuckled, pushing his hat back and leaning his chair on its hind legs. "For just a day, you can pretend you're coming back, too."

I shook my head and organized my paper notes in their drawer. "I'm happy for you, Gene, but I've really no desire to even pretend I'm going back. Those days are better behind me."

"Come on, Gin, don't tell me you've never wanted to go back to lemon cakes and Parisian dresses!" he laughed.

"Not one bit," I returned, jabbing my pen at him. "You can have the dresses in my stead. I leave them to you with no regrets."

"But really," he said, still grinning, "Don't you ever dream of going back? Marrying up, like me? Not having to work here anymore? Why, a lady of your class needn't work at all, like I'll have to!"

"Really and truly," I said. "I think I'd go mad without this work, even when it's as… harrowing as it has been this week." I stretched a little and indicated my clean desk with the pen. "This is what I live for now."

"You're crazy," he said. "And I mean that in the best possible way."

I laughed. "I'm not the one going back to tea parties and society columns. The record can show who's crazy and who's not."

He saluted me with a respectful wink, and we immersed ourselves in writing.

Thankfully, Mac was pleased with our work on the murder pieces and had let the ill-fated copper investigation go. It had been shrunk and relegated to a small article on the fifth page, while our stories were front page with bold headlines that, to be honest, I didn't much care for. But the content was my job, not the headlines, so I let it rest.

Halfway through the day, my morsie dinged. It was from Detective Ward.

<BODY FOUND STOP TULIP HAVEN STOP>

<QUERY DANCER STOP> I asked, tapping back. "Gene, we need to go to Tulip Haven. Do you know where that is? Is it another dance house?"

He stopped whatever he was doing with his newest gadget and frowned at me. "Yeah. It's over on the east side. Why? What happened?"

"Another murder," I said shortly, and my heart sank as I saw Ward's answer: <YES STOP SAME CASE STOP>

"This week's stories are becoming a series," I told Gene with regret. "I had hoped that Milly and Ludisia were the only ones."

Gene hefted his bag over his shoulder and pocketed his gadget and an autophone. "Murders happen every day, doll. We just have the privilege of not seeing every single one."

"I certainly feel as though we're getting more than our fair share, if that's the case," I said with a sigh.

"Hey, be glad Mac trusts you with the nasty stories now," he said, shooing me out the door. "Remember the old days?"

"I remember him entrusting me with nightmarish ones quite early," I retorted, checking my vest pockets. "Do you have another autophone?"

"Right here," he said, patting his jacket. "Out we go, then."

When we arrived at the Tulip Haven dance house, we met a very grim Detective Ward.

"Last night. Same method. No witnesses; no one heard anything out of the ordinary."

"Odd," I frowned. "Especially considering how loud it was when I heard it. Perhaps with all the storms lately, people are mistaking it for thunder? Do you have any leads on the weapon yet?"

"Not yet."

"Perhaps I can help, detective," Gene said brightly. "That's my area, after all."

Ward raised his eyebrows. "Really."

"Old family business," Gene said, adjusting the strap on his bag. "Or it would have been, anyway. Changed recently, thanks to my father."

"Over here," Ward gestured, herding us through the throng of people.

I thought I was hardened — at least slightly — to the sight and smell of faceless corpses, but this one pierced my heart just as the others had. There was something so very wrong about the anonymity… the way the killer erased the woman's personality, leaving only a naked, tattooed body behind. This woman's hair was dark and pulled back in an elegant bun, revealing a pink lily tattoo on her neck.

"What's this guy got against dancers, anyway?" muttered Gene. He wrinkled his nose and held his breath before leaning over to take a couple of snapshots.

"It's possible that the murderer is a woman," I said, trying to keep my stomach from purging its contents. "Perhaps she was jealous after finding her husband with too many lovers."

Ward was eying us carefully. "What do you think of the weapon?" he asked Gene.

Gene scratched his head. "Looks like one of the early offshoots of Van de Graaff's work. I'd heard that a Londoner — can't remember his name — was developing a sort of gun based on Graaff's direct current generator but changing the current to alternating so it could reach further. I didn't know anyone had been successful. You may need to focus your search on foreigners, Officer."

"Interesting," Ward muttered, studying him.

I usually went glassy-eyed when Gene started explaining electric machinery, but Ward seemed to have followed his reasoning.

"I wasn't aware that alternating current could create this effect," Ward said, motioning to the body. "Direct current using a battery seems more likely. I was thinking of interviewing the Vangees Company to see if they knew anything."

Gene shrugged. "I wouldn't if I were you. Waste of time. The developer I'm remembering had some interesting ideas with alternating current — very compelling, I'd say. Sounded promising." He took a few more photos as I asked Ward what time she'd been found and what theories he could share.

"As we cannot identify the victim as yet, we cannot determine a link between the victims. We believe she was a dancer at the Lily Bed," he pointed to her tattoo, "which could explain why people around here didn't hear a blast. She may not have been killed in this area. But currently we don't know for sure that this murder is even connected to the others. Could be a copy-cat."

"Or a coincidence?" I suggested.

He gave me a hard look.

"Oh yes," I paused in my note-taking. "You don't believe in coincidences."

"You can keep that part out," he said shortly.

I held up my pen in surrender.

"But you truly do not have any suspects, Detective?" I asked.

"We're pursuing several leads, including an old flame of one of the dancers. I —" His morsie dinged at that moment. "Excuse me," he said, pulling it out.

I took the moment to scribble some notes and inspect the scene, but turned abruptly when I heard Gene say, "What's up, Officer?"

Ward was scowling and tapping on his morsie. "Another murder."

I gave a tiny exclamation of dismay.

"Same kind?" asked Gene, putting away his camera and packing up.

Ward nodded, still tapping. "I need to go." He turned to his team and gave some directions in clipped tones. They listened soberly and saluted when he finished. He nodded to them, shook hands, and walked back to us. "Coming?"

I glanced at Gene. "Of course."

He nodded. "I have a bit of time before I'm expected elsewhere. Where we going, Officer?"

"Dahlia's," he said. "Dahlia's Delights. The victim is another dancer." His morsie pinged again. He tore the paper off and swore under his breath. "Pardon me, Miss Harper."

"What is it?" I asked, feeling trepidations.

"Two dancers at Dahlia's. Not one. They just found the other."

A familiar sensation of dread rose in me. In my five years at the *Journal*, I had yet to cover a story that involved five murders. Knowing that somewhere in our city lurked a killer who, for an unknown reason, had embarked on a killing spree of this magnitude in just three days chilled me to the bone. And why was the killer targeting dancers?

As we silently jogged the five blocks to Dahlia's, my heart pounded from more than our strenuous pace. Gene caught my elbow at one point when I stumbled while compulsively looking over my shoulder.

"You all right, Gin?" he asked under his breath.

I nodded.

He looked me over as we continued on. "You really shouldn't be on this story," he said, his lips pressed together in concern. "You're exhausted."

"I'm fine, Gene," I said, more sharply than I liked. "We need to get to the bottom of this. It's important."

"Someone else can do the digging, doll," he said, checking his watch. "It doesn't have to be you."

"I'm fine," I insisted. "Do you have an appointment?"

"Yeah, I'm expecting a message soon. Hey," he said, inspiration striking him, "Why don't you send Prudence a message? See if she has any ideas? I bet she could take over for a day or so."

I shook my head stubbornly, but then remembered that Prudence had hunted a story a year ago that involved a serial killer. Perhaps she could give me some pointers, and perhaps she could help me remain professional. I was feeling a little too personally involved. I took my morsie from my pocket as we neared Dahlia's and sent her a message:

<ON A HUNT WITH MULTIPLE MURDERS STOP I COULD USE YOUR EXPERTISE STOP ARE YOU AVAILABLE STOP>

"We're here," Ward called back to us. "You can follow me,

but stop when we arrive." He pointed. "I'm the first investigator, so you'll need to stay back from the scene."

Gene's pocket dinged. "Oops, that's it," he said. "I need to go. Are you sure you can handle this, Gin?"

"Go," I told him firmly, taking his proffered autophone and following Ward to the back. A moment later, we stood behind the dance house, looking down the alley at two more dead dancers, and my morsie pinged.

<FINISHING MY STORY FOR MAC STOP WILL TALK TO GENE ABOUT TAKING OVER FOR YOU STOP TAKE A BREAK STOP MUCH LOVE STOP>

I was irritated. Just because I was tired didn't mean I couldn't finish the story I'd discovered in the first place. I would have to have a talk with Gene and Pru later about their mother hen tendencies.

An officer speaking with Detective Ward interrupted my peeved thoughts.

"Turns out this body," the officer pointed to one of the dancers, who had red hair, "was actually at the Lily Bed, but the copper who called it in caught this fella dragging her over here. He said he 'found her' at the Lily Bed the next street over and was bringing her to the fuzz." The officer rolled his eyes. "Think we mighta found our hatchet man, Ward."

"Thank you, Jennings," Ward said.

The man in question sprang up at this and attempted to take Ward by the coat, except that two officers tackled him first.

"Sorry, sir," one said, wincing as the suspect's flailing arm caught him in the cheek. "Thought he was too drunk to stand."

"Never am I drunk!" the man yelled.

A likely story, I thought to myself, studying him. Though where he'd gotten his illegal alcohol was an idea for another story someday. How drunk had he been to drag a corpse in this condition through the street instead of running in the other direction when he found her?

Unfortunately, he caught me watching him and pointed to me, his eyes going in and out of focus.

"She knows! That dame there! She knows! I ain't drunk, 'mi, Miss? Mighta had some hooch, jus' a li'l, bu' ahm hittin' on all eight, yessir! I found tha' sheba there, yessir! I didn't do nothin' to 'er! Knew somefin was wrong all right, yessir, so I's bringin' 'er over here to this right buttons 'ere!" he gestured wildly to the officer who'd tackled him.

"I didn't find a weapon on him, sir," the officer said promptly. "She's cold, too, so if he killed her, it was quite a while before he dragged her over to me." He gave the suspect a look of disgust. "He would have had plenty of time to get this drunk after he murdered her and threw away the weapon. I have two guys at the Lily Bed looking for it, but they haven't found anything but stains and burn marks from the murder — and several bottles of gin."

The suspect raised one hand. "I'll sing." He waved four fingers toward Ward. "Two of them bottles is mine. Bu' none else. Nossir."

Ward was inspecting him with narrowed eyes. "Take him in, give him lots of water and some rest. Hopefully he'll remember something after he sobers up."

"You don't think he did it?" I said under my breath as an officer loaded him into the police wagon and another readied the horse.

"Too soon to know," he answered, frowning, but when he didn't think I was paying attention, I heard him mutter, "Not the right type. Not quite right." He moved past our group, inspecting the ground and walls of the buildings on either side and working his way toward the bodies.

Realizing Gene had taken the camera with him, I sighed and began taking notes instead. Using the autophone, I interviewed the officer who'd found the dancers and learned that he had just come upon the first dancer's body when he'd heard the drunkard stumbling down the street, cursing loudly and singing snatches of what could have been "Careless Love." He'd sent a message to Ward and radioed for support, then apprehended the drunk, who was carrying a woman who had been deceased for at least several hours.

Both dancers found by the officer were tattooed, as the other victims had been. The one he'd found here at Dahlia's had caramel skin and black hair with a dahlia on her breast, and the other, the dragged woman, had a tulip on her thigh. Both were without clothes and neither had been identified.

"Might take some time to identify them, too," the officer sighed and removed his hat to smooth his curly hair.

"Why?" I asked.

"Well, I was interviewing the girls at the other house yesterday, and they were telling me that several girls hadn't come into work — nervous about the murderer. Add that to the fact that their attendance is shoddy anyhow, the girls change their hair color often, there's a lot of turnover and moving between dance houses, and you get a rather tricky case. The first two at least were clothed distinctively and were identified by people who knew them. But with all the new immigrants coming to the city and managers who really don't care that much or keep tabs on their girls…" He shrugged.

How sad, I thought, suddenly thankful for Gene and even Mac. At least the people I worked with cared whether I lived or died.

"Thank you for speaking with me." I clicked off the autophone and put it away, noticing that Ward was bending beside the bodies, inspecting the hands and fingernails.

"Richards, did you move this body over here?"

Richards, the officer I'd been interviewing, looked embarrassed. "Yes sir. I thought it would be easier if they were together. I forgot what you said about moving bodies."

Ward looked stormy. "You might have erased evidence for this murder," he said, gesturing to the Dahlia dancer.

"Terribly sorry, sir." Richards was genuinely penitent. "Won't happen again."

"We'll need to talk to the dance house managers." Ward kept his voice even as he sketched the murder scene on a piece of paper. "Find out who's missing so we can identify the bodies. I'll go 'round to Baughmann's and ask him about weapons that might do this. All right then? When can we expect the coroner's report on these?"

"I talked to him," Jennings raised his hand. "He said with all these bodies you're sending him, it'll be Monday at least."

Ward opened his mouth, then saw me and changed his mind. "Heck," he said instead. "Well, do what you can. Lansing!" Another officer had just arrived. "I just did my inspection — double homicide, two locations. Bresden will fill you in. Want to do the secondary? I didn't check for prints yet."

The officer nodded and immediately approached the bodies the way Ward had, sometimes lying flat on the ground to investigate.

"I haven't met other detectives who invite the press to their murder scenes," I said quietly to Ward, voicing something I'd wondered the last couple hours. "Why do you?"

"I like to know what the public is going to read tomorrow," he said shortly.

"So you like to control the press."

"No," he said with a wry grin. "I like to know what the public will read of my investigation so that I know what my suspects will know." He eyed me for a moment. "And I like the way you present the case. I'd rather you be the first to get the details, so the public reads the version I prefer. So... yes. I suppose I do like a measure — a small measure — of control."

"Well then," I said dryly, "Would you like any other information to be in the paper tomorrow?"

He lifted his hat and rubbed his head. "The killer is using a specific method," he said slowly, his eyes focusing on something in the distance.

"You call that a *modus operandi*, correct?" I asked offhandedly, covering the fact that I'd been waiting for a chance to use the phrase ever since Pritchard had mentioned it a few months ago.

"Yes. The murderer is killing the dancers the same way, in alleys by dance halls, and usually in the evening or night. The only change we've noticed has been the lack of clothing on these latest victims. For now at least," he grimaced, "we have a specific type of murder that has occurred five times, and *that* may tell us something — or some things. Or we could be dealing with a copycat. For now, as I said, we are pursuing leads, and there is no need to panic. We are talking to the owners of the dance halls around town and warning their employees to be extra careful. As always, the public should be admonished to be wise and especially so at night." He stopped, glowering up at the sky, apparently thinking.

I waited.

"How do we track that weapon?" he muttered.

"Is that comment off the record?"

He jumped. "Yes. Naturally." He looked at me for a moment.

"How disgraceful was your fall from society, Miss Harper?"

I was startled. "Mid-grade, I would say. It was my choice of profession, nothing more."

His piercing eyes were considering me thoughtfully. "Do you know the Baughmann family?"

I shook my head. "Just Gene. He's their eldest. They're... not on the best of terms."

"Though that could change," he said under his breath. He

saw me staring at him and added, "I read the notice of his engagement the other day."

"Ah," I said awkwardly. "Yes, that may prove to smooth things over."

He was still frowning at me.

"Why do you ask?" I said, folding my hands and standing taller.

He shifted his gaze and waved to Richards, who was heading into Dahlia's to question the manager.

"You will recall, perhaps, that those of your upbringing are not necessarily welcoming to policemen — or detectives — entering their homes and questioning them. They find us rather vulgar, I believe?"

I blushed. "I —"

"It's all right, Miss Harper. I'm used to people finding my presence unwelcome." He grinned wryly. "People seem to consider it bad luck."

"Mostly just low-class." I winced. "But your way of speech must put them at ease. I've never heard a detective speak as —"

"Pretentiously?" he supplied. When I shook my head, he continued. "I've learned to adjust my speech to the beneficiary of my conversation." He gave me a crooked smile. "But the point is, Miss Harper, if you are available for an hour or so, I would be grateful if you would help me by accompanying me to the Baughmann home to... ease things over, if you will."

"Shall I change?" I asked ironically, putting away my pen and paper.

"It's more your manners that I could use," he said with nary an indiscreet glance at my garments. "And your credentials. Sometimes these businessmen like to be in the paper, said to be aiding in an investigation with their expertise."

"Excellent advertising," I said, catching on. I checked my watch. "Very well, Detective. I have not quite two hours to spare." As I put my watch away, I realized that my agreement was at least partially motivated by an innate curiosity to meet the family who had, like mine, disowned their offspring, and specifically, my reporting partner for the last five years. Yes, it would be quite fascinating to interview Edward Baughmann, I decided. I thought of sending Gene a message to tell him where I was headed but decided against it. We rarely threw salt on one another's wounds, no matter how old and partially scarred they were.

The afternoon was cloudless, and as we made our way to the Hill, I found myself enjoying the walk, despite its grave purpose.

"Have you been back much?" Ward asked as we drew near the Hill, watching a car of society-goers pass us.

"To my old home?" I asked. "No, not at all."

He raised his eyebrows.

"My family isn't what you would call forgiving." I snorted quietly. "Or lenient."

"I see," he said. He glanced sideways at me. "It doesn't seem to have hurt you."

I cocked my head at him. "I suppose that depends on which way you mean. Their response was expected, so it did not hurt as it could have. I had been hurt by them more deeply for much longer. It was rather a relief to have the final blow done."

He paused. Though his eyes were shuttered, I could predict what he was thinking.

"Were you working at this precinct about seven years ago?" I asked.

"No. The war," he said shortly.

"Right. Yes. Sorry."

"What would I know if I had?" he asked, giving me another sideways glance.

I watched a garish pink automobile rounding the corner and felt torn about whether to commit to this conversation I'd so recklessly started. "It depends which paper you would have been reading."

"All of them. I read all the papers."

When I favored him with a look of disbelief, he looked straight back. "Truly, though, Miss Harper. Anything could be related to a case I'm working."

"Well then," I said, wondering if I dared to go on. "You might have seen an article about the son of a society man... committing suicide." I swallowed. He was watching me silently. "I was there, and it wasn't suicide."

"And your family was complicit."

"After the fact, when I told them the truth," I said, even now feeling hot rage in my veins, tinged with the memory of shame and fear. "They wouldn't allow me to... to tell what had happened."

"But you see it still," he said with unexpected insight.

"Yes," I whispered. "And..."

"And so you don't go back."

"Yes."

He tugged me to the side, around a pile of horse leavings.

"High society can sometimes think of the common man as that," I said, pointing to what we'd missed, "but being part of a poorer class is freedom for me."

He nodded thoughtfully. "It's given you freedom and clarity, if I'm not mistaken."

"Yes."

"This young man. Was he your fiancé?"

"No. But... he was a… a good friend. Someday, perhaps…" The ache rose up in me, the ache that I'd felt whenever I hadn't been with Nathaniel, the ache that had swallowed my whole being when he'd died.

"And his 'crime' against his attacker?"

"Same as mine," I said. "Leaving. Only... he died for it."

"And you are left to live."

Hearing my greatest guilt out loud for the first time, my

eyes filled instantly, and I whipped out my handkerchief. "I'm sorry," I said, utterly discomfited. When I dared to raise my blushing face, I saw him looking discreetly away.

My focus shifted off myself and onto a soldier turned detective. "You understand, don't you?"

He didn't answer. We traversed the entire block before he cleared his throat and spoke.

"I'm terribly sorry, Miss Harper. Very unprofessional of me to inquire into your personal life."

"It's all right," I said, squaring my shoulders. "That'll be their house, then?" I pointed up the street to the address he'd indicated at the beginning of our trek.

"Yes. Right this way."

When I look back on it, I realize that this conversation marked the beginning of an unlikely friendship between Detective Ward and me. Nothing more was said, but as we ascended the steps to the mansion that used to house my assistant, I felt the same sureness, the same ease and trust that I had felt these five years with Gene, and I was happy.

8

The Baughmanns' butler opened the fancy mahogany door. His face was slack with boredom, but he brightened at the sight of us.

"What may I do for you?" he asked, fixing his jacket and staring keenly at Ward's proffered badge that promised interesting happenings to follow our entrance.

"We'd like to see Mr. Baughmann, if he's home," Ward said.

"He's at luncheon with Mrs. Baughmann," the butler answered, his eyes begging us to stay.

"We'll gladly wait," I put in helpfully.

He beamed. "Right through here into the parlor, ma'am... sir... I'll let him know you're here." He stopped halfway out the parlor door and turned around. "What sort of business do you have with the master, Officer...?"

"Detective Ward," he supplied, sitting in a large armchair and putting his feet up. "We're here to beg his expertise. It's about the Blaster Murders."

I winced at the use of the headline. Not my first choice.

The butler's face shone with glee. "Of course, sir. Right away, Detective sir."

"I get the feeling not much happens around here," Ward said idly, looking around at the family portraits and knick-knacks that filled the gloomy room.

"He's probably new," I said, picking at a thread in the armchair I had chosen. It felt strange to be surrounded by such finery again. I shifted uneasily against the overstuffed cushions and glared at the gilded mirror across from me.

"It's been a while, eh?" said Ward. His face was hidden under his hat, and his fingers were laced over his chest. He leant back and appeared to be primed for a nap.

I gestured rudely at him to relieve my feelings, and though I was sure he couldn't see me, I noticed a faint smile flit across his face.

"It will be quite a wait, won't it?" he asked.

"Undoubtedly," I said. "He'll want to make sure we know our place."

Completely to my surprise, the parlor door opened at that moment, and in strode a tall, suave man in his late sixties with a white goatee that he was smoothing anxiously now. I recognized Gene's aquiline nose and broad shoulders.

"Ah, Detective."

Ward removed his hat and stood, looking not a bit sheepish. They shook hands, and then Baughmann turned to me.

"And — I'm very sorry, but I'm not sure who you are."

I had risen to my feet and now held out my hand. "Ginnie Harper," I said. "Reporter for the *Franklin Journal*. If you don't mind, I'll record this interview."

If I was expecting a chilly reception based on my low-class city newspaper, I was surprised once again. He took my hand and daintily kissed it, assenting to the recording and entreating us to be seated once more. I carefully set up the autophone, speaking quietly to program my voice and offering it to Ward to do the same. Then I left the program button on as

Baughmann offered us refreshments, and switched it to record once we'd accepted.

Baughmann rang a bell and gave an order to the young butler, who tried to remain as long as possible before reluctantly heading back to the kitchen. "My man told me you were here about the murders. A terrible thing. How may I be of assistance?"

"It's the weapon," Ward said as he took out his oversized morsie. "We don't know what it could be. Perhaps you've read about the effects?"

"Yes, yes, I did," he answered, looking agitated. "I subscribe to your *Franklin Journal*," he nodded to me, "and I've been appalled — absolutely appalled. What a frightful crime!" He crossed his legs and then uncrossed them.

"There have been three more murders," Ward said. "Today."

Baughmann smoothed his goatee again, his eyes horrified. "All with the same type of weapon? The… blasting, I believe they called it?" He turned to me for confirmation. I nodded.

"I have pictures, if you can stomach them," Ward said, leaning forward and holding out some snapshots. "If you're willing, I'd like you to take a look and tell me what you think could have caused this type of injury."

"Naturally, naturally," Baughmann said. He hesitated, then gathered his courage and took the photographs, studying each one with a blanched face. We waited as he cleared his throat and handed them back. "How —" his voice cracked, and he started over. "*Ahem.* How loud was it?"

Ward blinked. "The discharging of the weapon?"

"Yes. What sort of sound?"

"It was a loud crack," I said, and he turned to me. "A loud crack," I repeated. "I was there the first time it happened, near the alley." I thought back for a moment. "It reverberated off the buildings — quite startling. I'm uncertain how else to describe it."

"There were no witnesses to the other deaths," Ward added, "so Miss Harper is the best one to tell you."

Baughmann clasped his hands. "The blackening, the charring, the burned effect — all isolated to the face. It's a new weapon, very new. I've not heard of it. Perhaps you know that my company refrained from entering a weapons contract? I've kept up on the latest developments, however, and I know of nothing that would cause this."

"Can you tell us what type of weapon it could be?" asked Ward, tapping into his morsie. "Anything would help."

Baughmann closed his eyes and leaned back with a furrowed brow. "It would have to produce a concentrated beam of electric current — definitely direct current — to have such a localized effect. It would require a battery, I assume…"

"Size?" Ward prompted, tapping rapidly.

"Hard to say. If the inventor found a way to make the battery small enough, the weapon could fit into a hand, into a pocket. It certainly wouldn't have to be bulky."

I paused in my note-taking and thought about the sound of pounding feet I'd heard in the alley after Ludisia was killed. The blaster would have to be small, I thought, for someone to carry it away with that much speed. And others surely would have noticed someone fleeing with a large object at that time of night if it had been of substantial size. Baughmann must be right.

The idea was horrifying: why, the murderer could be walking around with the death-gadget in his pocket at this moment, ready to pull it out at his leisure! I shuddered.

Baughmann noticed my movement. "Quite right, Miss Harper, quite right. No one should have access to such a device. No good can come of it. I would urge you to speak to Yuri Morislav, but I can tell you with surety that he will know nothing of it. One thing I admire about the man is his intent for the good of humanity: and we know by reading your articles that nothing about this weapon will benefit mankind."

He was right, I thought. Though the murderer may think that he was benefitting himself in some dreadful way, he was only harming himself as well. One cannot take the life of another — especially with malicious intent — without reaping terrible consequences to the soul.

Ward was perusing his notes. "And you are quite certain that the current would be direct, not alternating? Do I have reason to interview the Vangees?"

Baughmann looked surprised. "That little plant that pursues outdated ideas? I wouldn't think… well, but yes, they manufacture the Stunners, which are being widely used, so perhaps they could be of service to you."

"I ask because I was told definitively by another source to look at alternating current operators instead," Ward said.

Baughmann shook his head. "Unless I have missed some recent development, I would have to disagree with your source."

Ward considered him for a moment. I had the distinct impression that he was weighing him on a well-used scale in his mind. "Would you keep that opinion if you knew that the other source was your son?"

"My son?" He seemed flabbergasted. "You've spoken with James? He isn't even interested in electricity — he's studying chemistry abroad! Why on earth —"

"He means Eugene," I interrupted, my stomach tightening.

His face turned slightly red, and he sat back in his chair as if he'd been slapped. "Eugene."

"Perhaps you are aware that he works for the *Journal*?" asked Ward. "He gave me his opinion on the weapon after seeing the second body."

"You work with Gene?" Baughmann ignored Ward and turned to me. I was surprised by the wistful look in his eyes.

"Ye-es," I said doubtfully.

"How is he?" he asked quietly.

"Quite well," I said. "Engaged, as I'm sure you are aware."

His hand fluttered before squeezing the armchair. "Yes, yes, I read that."

"Have you changed your opinion on the current?" Ward asked again.

Baughmann came out of a reverie. "What's that? The current? Yes. I mean, no, I would not. It's definitely a direct current weapon." It was clear that his focus was no longer on the matter we'd come to discuss.

"Would you… would you be so kind…" He swallowed and looked at me. "Would you tell him that his mother would like to see him?"

Though my prejudice against him for my friend's sake was still strong, my heart went out to this white-haired father against my will.

"Certainly," I stammered.

Ward asked him another question, and he turned away from me, but I found that I could not give my full attention to their conversation. I was thinking of my own father. Was his beard white now as well? And my mother: did she long to see me? Had they since repented of their decision to cast me out? Or had they lavished their attention instead on my younger sister? Was she now a well-bred jewel of whom they could finally be proud? For all that I had been moved by Mr. Baughmann's show of yearning, my heart told me that the latter scenario was far more likely for my family. I gave myself a little shake and shifted my focus back to what Ward was saying.

"Thank you very much for your time, Mr. Baughmann. I hope we have not inconvenienced you."

"Not at all, not at all. I'm happy to be of help — though I doubt I've done much for your investigation."

"You've narrowed my search," said Ward. "I'm much obliged to you. Thank you for the names of these manufacturers." He patted his breast pocket where his morsie was lodged.

"Quite all right," said Baughmann distractedly. He took my hand as we turned to leave. "Thank you for news of Gene. I do hope you'll pass along my regards to him — and my congratulations."

"Of course," I said, withdrawing my hand to turn off the autophone and stow it in my pocket.

The door closed behind us, and we walked away, ignoring the curious faces of the butler and cook at the kitchen window.

"He gave you more manufacturers?" I asked, taking out my pad of paper.

"Yes." Ward helped me navigate the steps leading down to the street as I scribbled. "I doubt we'll find anything with them, but perhaps they can start me on the right path."

"You don't think a company is making these devices?"

"No. I think the murderer is quite ingenious. I think it's a private weapon. You'll notice that both Baughmanns, though they disagree on the design, have seen nothing like it in development. But of course, they — or I — could be wrong."

"That doesn't narrow it down either," I said, my heart sinking. "This city is full of individual inventors."

Ward nodded. "Luxity seems to breed them, doesn't it? Though it's likely that the murderer works for a manufacturer: he would then have access to parts." His pocket dinged, and he removed the slip of paper from his morsie. "One of the dancers was identified," he muttered. He quickly tapped a reply. I waited until he slid it back into his pocket.

"Detective, would it perhaps be quicker to pursue the murderer's motivation than to track the weapon?"

"If we had any idea at all what that was, then yes," Ward said dryly. "Though we're pursuing a few ideas, I think we have a better chance of catching him with the guard I've set up around the dance halls throughout the city. We're using several methods, you see."

"Are the guards uniformed and armed?" I asked, scribbling.

"Plains clothes and yes." He frowned. "That's not for the record, Miss Harper. Our murderer likely is following your story in the *Journal*."

"Personal notes." I smiled.

"Just keep them that way."

"What weapons do they carry?"

Ward seemed to consider whether he should answer my question. "It's a new manufacture. Baughmann just mentioned it actually — the Vangees Stunner. It uses electrical shock to paralyze the perpetrator long enough to take him into custody."

"Lasting effects?"

He shook his head. "That's the best part. Non-lethal, but completely effective. I have one here, if you'd like to see it." He took from his trouser pocket a small silver device.

I refrained from touching it. "How does it work?"

"One simply presses this button, and the electricity emits from this end. I've kept my revolver, of course, but the Stunner is a handy gizmo."

"Quite ingenious," I remarked. "I think I'd like one for myself."

"Better than knives?" he asked mildly.

"How—"

"Did I know?" he finished. "The art of observation, Miss Harper, cannot be underestimated." He gestured to my boot. "Do you really think you can remove it quickly enough once you are attacked?"

Irritated, and goaded into proving myself, I glanced around the street to be sure no one was watching and then kicked my foot up behind my back, slid the knife from it in a swift motion, and held it to his side — whereupon I found my wrist clamped in a very firm grip.

"I concede," he said. "You are very speedy." He released my wrist gently, and I replaced the blade, feeling anything but speedy.

"Did you learn that block in the war?" I asked before I thought better of it.

"War certainly toned my reflexes," he admitted, not seeming to mind the question. "But I've had plenty of practice in my current line of work as well."

My pocket dinged, and I was glad of the distraction to check the paper printing from my morsie.

\<AT THE OFFICE STOP WHERE ARE YOU STOP MAC WANTS AN UPDATE STOP\>

\<ON MY WAY STOP\> I tapped.

"Gene is expecting me at the *Journal*," I said to Ward.

"Allow me to walk you there?"

"If you've time," I said.

"Of course. I hope you have enough material for your article," he said as we turned onto a noisy street just down the Hill. "I'd hate to think I wasted your afternoon."

"Not at all. It's been very productive."

"Good. For me as well."

"We make an effective team." I smiled.

"It certainly seems that way. Though I could do with less of your 'tell the public everything' opinion."

"And I with your 'keep the masses in ignorance.'"

He shrugged. "To each his own, it seems."

"Live and let live," I agreed.

We walked in companionable silence the rest of the way to the *Journal*, where I was greeted by an impatient Gene and an apoplectic Mac.

9

"Where have you been?" Gene whispered as he escorted me to Mac's office. "Mac's been in one of his rages all morning — asked where you were fifteen times — I swear."

"I wasn't supposed to be back until now," I argued, checking my watch. "I'm right on time."

"You know Mac's version of 'right on time.'" Gene rolled his eyes. "If you're not here when he wants you, you might as well be later than Prudence! And speaking of Prudence, you're not to work this case for a few more days, you hear? I talked to her, and she's got some great ideas. You take a break and work out the kinks in your forehead."

I rubbed the offending portion of my anatomy and frowned at him, creating more wrinkles. "We should talk about that. I told you I didn't need her to take over."

"Let's talk about it later," he whispered as we approached Mac's door. I could hear him roaring inside. "For now, just don't get him angrier than he already is."

The noise within peaked as we opened the door.

"I told that bluenose I'd have nothing to do with him, and I meant it!" He was shouting into his telephone and punctuating his words with his sausage fingers. "You can tell him to buzz off and quit calling here or else!" He slammed the receiver down and glared at us. "Sit down! Harper! Where have you been? What about my deadline?"

"I've got the draft right here," I said soothingly, pulling it out. "And—"

"None of that!" he snapped. "Let me have it."

We sat silently as if on pins until he finished scanning it. "What about the new murders? Baughmann here told me there've been three more!"

"Yes sir, I was about to tell you—"

"Then tell me already, Harper! And write it! What's the good of telling me when we get paid to tell the public? Get out of here!" He picked up the phone again and dialed. "Operator! Get me Westinghouse! And you!" he pointed to Gene and me. "I thought I told you to get out!"

Out we accordingly went, leaving no room for further demonstrations of verbal abuse.

"I told you," Gene gasped, closing the door behind him and leaning against it. "Where were you?"

"At your father's place," I said, angered into telling him after all. "Ward wanted more leads on the weapon."

Gene groaned. "So you went there? For Pete's sake, Gin!"

I trotted down the hallway, irritated. "It was a solid lead. And why did you tell Ward it was alternating current when it clearly wasn't?"

"So that's what Dad told you, huh?" Gene said darkly, catching up with me.

"Yes. He said investigating the Vangees could be helpful — or I surmised that, anyhow," I amended.

Gene snorted. "Of course he did. They're business rivals. You know how this works, Gin."

We stopped at our desk. "Are you saying he misled us? He told me to tell you that your mother wants to see you. He seemed... sad that you don't go back."

Gene sat down wearily and took my hand to pull me down, too. "Sit, Gin. You look exhausted. And don't tell me you're fine — I know what this case is doing to you." He rubbed his head. "I'm sorry I yelled at you, and I'm sorry I talked to Pru without you. The truth is, I hate seeing how much of a toll this case is taking on you. You're a good person; you're not meant to see stuff like this. And you're too good to be lied to. I hate that you had to see my father. He seems like such a nice old man, doesn't he? So worried about his poor, estranged son, so eager to cooperate with the law and do everything he can for you? I don't blame you for being taken in."

"What do you mean?"

He leaned back in his chair and ran a hand through his hair. "Remember how it is? These games we'd all play? You may have forgotten, but I haven't. I'm going back, after all. The *game*, Gin, the game where you look a certain way and talk a certain way and act good and kind and gracious… and then you brutally knock it all down when it suits you. Lies don't mean a thing there — it's all lies. You lie to do business, you lie to your wife, your wife lies to you. You lie to your kids to keep the peace, you lie to your friends to look better, you lie to your doctor to get the medicine you want. Come on, Gin! Remember that web? Remember how to traverse it? Your business is doing well, but another small business in town has a product that's rapidly gaining popularity. What if they become a real rival? Much better to throw suspicion on them through a murder scandal."

I lifted my shoulders and dropped them again in exhaustion. Perhaps he was right — perhaps I was too tired, not cut out for this hunt. He was reminding me of the very reason I'd left my own family.

"Why do you want to go back?"

"Because I can do good in that web, Gin!" He leaned

forward earnestly. "I can use those resources to improve, to invent! I know how to make my way."

"And you act like I'm crazy to stay here," I said, shaking my head. "At least I know where I stand."

"Even with Mac yelling at you?" He gave me a brief grin.

"Especially with Mac yelling at me." I sighed. "Speaking of which, I need to type up the interviews from this afternoon."

"Here," he said, holding out his hand. "I'll help. We'll get it all done so quickly Mac will be speechless — at least for a couple minutes."

"Too good to hope for," I muttered, already typing rapidly. "But at least we won't be on the chopping block."

"You'll be careful, won't you?" He was looking at me with genuine worry in his eyes. "I know all these dames were dancers, but I still don't like the idea of you poking into back alleys."

"I know, Gene." My eyes were on the lines of black letters being punched into the white paper. "I'm always careful."

"If there are no more murders, you could take a break for a couple of days, process things a bit. You know, do some lady stuff or something."

I couldn't help but chuckle. "Like get my nails done?" I held up an ink-stained finger for his perusal while typing with the other hand.

"Sure." He laughed. "They could use it."

"We'll see," I said noncommittally. "But thanks, Gene, really."

"Your friends are here for you. Never forget that." He gave me a smile, then got to work transcribing notes. We typed in a comfortable cacophony, listening to several bongs of the clock striking over us, as the newsroom slowly emptied.

When at last we presented our finished article to Mac for the morning paper, he grudgingly admitted it was "good enough" and pointed us out the door with his "ready for the press" expression.

Gene walked me to my apartment.

"Have a good night," he called, "and think about my offer!"

I lifted a hand in goodbye as I opened my door. "For now, I'm just going to get a good night's sleep. Hopefully."

"Yes. Do that."

"Good night."

I closed my door and let myself sink slowly, like molasses, into my chair. Suddenly too tired to even make dinner, I gnawed on some stale crackers in a tin by my chair and checked my morsie absently as the light filtering through the windows dimmed.

<ARE YOU HUNGRY STOP SOMETHING I WANT TO DISCUSS STOP MELS DINER STOP IF YOU DONT MIND STOP>

I paused my gnawing. *If you don't mind?* Rather polite for the reticent detective. Ward *was* talking about the case, wasn't he? I was hungry, clearly, but not for romantic overtures. Those required a rational mind and playful mood, neither of which I could garner at the moment.

"But Ginnie dear," I told myself with a tired little laugh, "you're flattering yourself too much." I took myself in hand. "Why would Ward want to woo you over dinner after viewing dead bodies together this afternoon? He just wants to discuss the case."

I chewed another cracker and, despite myself, started salivating as I thought of the crispy potatoes at Mel's.

How would it look? An unwed, female reporter out at dinner with a detective?

"You're not sixteen anymore," I argued, shaking my cracker at the little mirror on my wall. "You don't need a chaperone for an outing with a man." I gave myself a fierce scowl. "And why are you acting as if people in this part of the city care? It's the modern age, for goodness' sake. Your high society airs are showing."

I turned the cracker over in my hands a few times, staring at the conflicted hazel eyes in the mirror.

"Focus on what's important," I murmured. "If Detective Ward needs to discuss the murderer, then you ought to do what you can to help him."

With that decided, I stood and straightened my vest, picked up my coat, and left my apartment with only one more glance in the mirror to fix my errant hair.

As I walked from one lamppost to the next, another thought struck me. Prudence lived two blocks down from Mel's Diner — on my way. What if I stopped in and brought her with me? I breathed a relieved sigh at the thought. The plan satisfied all my concerns. Detective Ward, if he had any ulterior motives, would be deflected by the presence of a friend, better even than a chaperone, and because Pru had worked on serial murder stories before, she could lend her insight to the discussion. I retrieved my morsie from my pocket and rapidly tapped a message.

<DO YOU WANT DINNER STOP MELS DINER STOP DISCUSS MY STORY STOP>

As I reached her door, I received her reply.

< SO SORRY STOP IM AWFUL SICK STOP NOT TONIGHT STOP TALK TOMORROW STOP>

Concerned, I knocked gently and then stood on my tiptoes, un-wedged her key, and walked in, placing the key on her table.

"Pru?" I called softly. "I'm sorry you're not well. Can I bring you something from the diner? Some soup?"

The apartment was dark. I gestured impatiently, initiating the ceiling lights, which flared to life in an extravagant sun pattern. I blinked, my eyes adjusting to the sudden contrast.

"Pru?" I tripped over a boot. "I'd be happy to bring you something."

Making my way into the kitchen, I gagged at the smell of decaying food. It looked as though she hadn't washed her dishes or thrown away her spoiled milk on the worktable since my last visit. How could she live like this? I wondered, not for the first time. I pinched my nose and went back to the single bedroom.

"Pru?" I waved on the corner light. "I know you're awake because you just —"

She wasn't there.

I stopped short. "Pru?" A horrible feeling made me freeze and then whirl around, my breath caught in my throat.

Nothing happened. Feeling stupid and frightened, I searched the apartment, knowing I was stalling for time while I ran through scenarios in my head.

<WHERE ARE YOU STOP>

I stood in the living room, surrounded by clothing and refuse, waiting for her answer.

<HOME STOP DONT COME STOP DONT WANT YOU TO GET SICK STOP ITS REALLY HORRIBLE STOP AND MY KEY IS GONE STOP"

A phantom of unreality drifted its shaky fingers over me. I began to tremble. My eyes scanned the room. There was the set of Pru's favorite boots — where they had been Wednesday, lying against the sofa. The untouched food… the spoiled milk… the green hat that she always wore for luck on a difficult hunt — lying on the kitchen floor. The kitchen floor that was spotless, in odd contrast to the disgusting smell and cluttered cabinet top and worktable.

I fled the phantom and ran to Mel's Diner as if those cold, ghostly fingers were clutched around my neck.

10

I did my best to maintain a semblance of composure as I entered the bright, warm interior of the diner. The noisy chatter of the customers and the swishing skirts of the waitresses assaulted me with normalcy. I forced my breathing to slow and frantically cast my eyes around the room.

"Ward!" I whispered. I threaded my way through the crowded tables to where he was sitting, engrossed in the latest issue of *Current News*. Glancing up and catching sight of me, he rose with a welcoming hand, but in my agitation, I neither took his hand nor sat down. He frowned.

"Miss Harper, what's wrong?"

"I was just at Prudence's house," I said, taking hold of the table to steady myself. "She wasn't there, and I'm horribly afraid she hasn't been there and that something dreadful has happened to her."

"Sit," he ordered, drawing me down to sit at the booth. "You're white as chalk. Start from the beginning."

He gestured to the waitress, who had just wandered our way. "A soda for my friend, please. Fried chicken?" he asked me. I made a restless movement with my hand. "Chicken," he said more firmly. "With fries, please." When she moved away, he leaned toward me. "You went to her house this evening. Continue."

Feeling like vomiting, I pushed down my fear, concentrated on his solid presence, and related what I had found.

"You said that she sent you a message yesterday," he said.

"Yes, yes, she did — or someone did." With shaking hands, I handed him the message that had printed at Pru's apartment. I realized I was shivering uncontrollably. "This is the message I just received — while standing in her living room."

His eyes narrowed as he read it. He pulled out his morsie and began tapping. Without looking up, he handed me his coat. "Put that on. You've had a shock. So you have no confirmation of her actual whereabouts since Tuesday, when you saw her in her apartment?"

I nodded, drawing the bulky coat around myself, feeling warmth soak into my trembling body. The scent of aftershave and cedar surrounded me, joining the homey smells of the diner and calming me.

"So. We have two rather obvious options here. First, we do not know where Miss Bailey is. Either she is lying to you or someone else is sending you messages from her device — for what purpose, we do not know."

"We don't know if she is even alive." I released the words of my fear from the cave-like comfort of his coat.

"We also must not jump to conclusions. We must investigate." He looked me over, frowning. "Can you give me directions to her apartment? You can eat; I'll take you home, and then I'll go see what I can find."

"I'll come with you," I said.

He considered me for a moment, taking in my wounded-animal posture. I braced myself for an argument.

"All right," he said instead. "Will you eat first or bring the food?"

"I'll bring it," I said as it fortuitously arrived. I dumped the warm, greasy contents unceremoniously into my handkerchief as Ward paid the bill and we left.

"Oh! Here," I said, removing his coat as we stepped out into the chilly night air. He gave me another of his piercing looks before taking it from me.

"Miss Harper, you must stay behind me at all times. Because we don't know what is happening or where Miss Bailey is, we are walking into an unknown and potentially dangerous situation. You must do exactly as I say as I say it. Do you understand?"

I nodded, squaring my shoulders. Going back to the apartment to find answers somehow made me feel calmer, especially since I was not alone this time. A growling protest emitted from my stomach, and I blushed, retrieving a piece of chicken for dinner on the way.

The two blocks of walking allowed me to finish the chicken and half the fries, but when I saw her door, my appetite was suddenly gone. "Here," I said, willing my voice to be steady and pointing to her door. "The key is at the top of the doorframe."

He reached up and felt around. "I most sincerely hope you do not imitate her security measures," he muttered.

"I don't have the same problem of losing everything I own," I retorted shakily, trying to keep my voice light.

Ward was still groping for the key.

"Here," I said, gesturing him aside and standing on tiptoe, "I know where it —"

It wasn't until I felt the crack and even pushed my finger part of the way into it that I remembered where I'd left it.

"It's inside on the table," I said, my voice very sheepish. "I left without locking the door. I was so—"

But Ward had just tried the handle, and the door remained stubbornly closed. He glanced down the hall, feeling around the doorframe and checking the floor.

"Come with me," he said shortly, and jogged down the hallway back outside. Looking over his shoulder to be sure I was there, he circled the building, staring up at the fire escapes and down the alleyway. When we'd made a full circle, he came back around to her door.

"You have her permission to enter her apartment, correct?" he asked, taking out a small pouch.

"Yes, that's partially why the key is there," I said. "What —?"

With quick, sure movements, he picked the lock and swung the door open, holding me back and staying to the side. After a moment, he carefully entered. The lights were on; I had not taken the time to turn them off when I made my hasty exit. The only sound was muffled noise from the streets; I realized I was holding my breath. I went immediately to the table and found what I'd feared: the key was gone. Ward was creeping around, eyes taking in everything from the stained ceiling to the clothing-covered floor. His Stunner was in his hand. Seeing this, I removed my knife from my boot and followed in his wake. When we entered the kitchen, I tripped over the same malevolent boot from earlier in the evening. To catch my balance, I grabbed the cabinet top, sending a cascade of dirty dishes to the floor. The clatter almost hid the sound of the window in the bedroom opening, but the squeak at the end came just as the dishes settled.

"The bedroom," I whispered.

Ward ran the way I pointed, gesturing me to stay back.

A cold draft greeted us as Ward opened the door and waved on the light. He scanned the empty room and then raced to the window, where I cautiously joined him. We could see a dark shape hastily dropping from the last rung of the fire escape onto the ground in the alleyway. As the person jumped, a spark fell from the metal ladder.

"Blast," Ward muttered and blew his whistle. "Stay here,"

he said, and lifted himself out the window, navigating the fire escape and dropping to the ground with ease.

I watched until he disappeared around the corner, then went to wait at the door.

Ward returned a few minutes later with tense shoulders and a grim tilt to his mouth.

"Did that look like Prudence?" he asked me as I shut the door behind him.

I shook my head. "I couldn't tell. She often wears trousers on a hunt, and she's tall, so it's hard to tell if it was her or a man."

"Could she have made that jump?" he asked.

"Yes," I said. "She's done much riskier things. But she wouldn't run from me… unless she saw you and thought you were an intruder? I don't know. I don't think it was her. Her movements…" I trailed off. My mind was racing. "Do you smell that?" I asked suddenly. We both turned to the kitchen.

Ward opened Pru's old-fashioned wood-burning stove and gave a grunt.

"Tongs," he told me, but we both knew it was too late. The smoking remnants in the oven were ashes. If they'd contained any information that would be helpful to us, they were gone now. One little white piece that he pulled out with the tongs I offered was tantalizingly blank, telling us simply that the ashes were from burned paper.

We sat back on the floor, disappointed. Ward studied the kitchen from our vantage point, then slowly crawled across the floor and to the right.

"Here," he said, pointing.

I moved to his side, where he was contemplating a spot on one of her dirty cupboards near the floor. Her cabinets were suffering from the same neglect as most of her kitchen, but the area that Ward was eying was different.

"You see it?" he asked me.

I nodded. "It's been scrubbed."

He was still squatting, frowning at the spot. Slowly, methodically, he examined all the surfaces at waist level and below until he reached a wall that made him stop.

"Not blood," he muttered, studying something I couldn't see. "It's too orange. But what?"

I leaned down next to him and scrutinized the small reddish-orange smear, barely hidden by the shadow of the cabinet next to it. Recognition sparked in my mind.

"Henna," I said. "I think it's henna."

I retrieved the little box from the worktable and brought it to him. He lifted a smidgeon of the green powder from the box and rubbed it between his fingers quizzically. Instead of explaining, I too took a pinch, added water from the sink, and then smudged it onto the wall. The stains were identical.

"Excellent work." He studied the box. "This is used for dying hair?"

"Yes. Pru is a trifle obsessed. She was dying her hair with it Tuesday when I saw her here."

He replaced the box on the worktable and stared into the distance. I watched, wondering where his mind was taking him, and if it would lead us to the answer. The questions in this kitchen would stifle me if I let them, so I kept them at bay by taking out my ever-comforting pad of paper and firmly jotting down notes, practically engraving my words into the paper. The focused quiet of the room continued for a minute more. Then Ward spoke.

"Look for a rag or a mop. And put your gloves on, please."

We searched through closets and cabinets and wastebaskets and even under the bed. I found a rag in the sink, but the red on it turned out to be henna once more. We found nothing.

"Outside," Ward said. A memory triggered in my mind.

"On the fire escape, the bottom platform that you skipped. There was another cloth!"

Losing no time, he climbed through the window for the

second time that night. The cold air made me shiver as I watched him descend into the darkness. When he reappeared on the fire escape in front of me, he was triumphantly holding a stained rag.

"Must've dropped it on the way down." His eyes were sparking with what I recognized in journalists as the look of the Hunt.

We returned to the kitchen, where he removed a small bottle and syringe from his coat pocket.

"What is that?" I whispered as he unscrewed the top and dipped the syringe inside.

"Hydrogen peroxide," he answered, squatting down and letting a couple drops fall onto the brown-stained rag which he'd placed on the floor. "I learned about it in Germany during the war. I keep it with me for just this purpose. If this is blood, it will—" He smiled grimly as the rag bubbled. "It will do that." He pulled out his morsie and began tapping. "I'm opening an investigation. It may be too early to tell, but I am quite certain that there has been foul play here. I'm sorry, Miss Harper, for what this may mean for your friend. Please try not to jump to conclusions. We don't know whose blood this is." He put away his morsie and peered at the saturated cloth on the floor. We were silent, contemplating the amount of liquid that it had soaked up. "When do you normally speak to Miss Bailey?"

"Do you mean what time of day?"

He nodded.

"When we worked together, we spoke at the office during the day. When she was on an extended story, we sent messages at different times during the day or in the evening."

"Would you ever send her a message during the night?" he asked, glancing out the window into the dark street.

I hesitated. "No… she would, but I would not."

He took a breath and let it out; his eyebrows knotted. "Well, then. If you will consent, I would like to use your relationship with her to draw out whoever has her morsie. Tomorrow, I would like you to send her a message. I will give you the wording after I think about it some more. Perhaps we can discover the answer to this riddle. Will you do it?"

"Yes," I said. "As soon as you think of it."

"I want you to act as you always do," Ward said. "Do and say nothing you wouldn't normally." He checked his watch. "In fact, you ought to go home. We don't know if the intruder saw you, so acting as you would on a typical evening would be best." He paused, seemingly divided in his mind. "I would like you to have accompaniment home, just in case the perpetrator saw you." He paused again. "I'll send the night patrol with you when he gets here. He can stay on your street tonight. Do you have anyone else who could stay with you?"

I thought about it and shook my head. "Pru is the only one I can think of. I'm not close with anyone else… except Gene." I blushed. "And that would hardly be appropriate."

"Well, then." He considered me. "Lock your door and windows, Miss Harper. And sleep with your knife nearby."

There was a knock at the door. "That will be him," he said, getting up and slipping the bottle and syringe into his coat pocket. I stood in the kitchen, hugging myself and wishing that I could stay to watch the investigation instead of going home to my bed, where I'd likely toss and turn all night.

When the night patrolman, who turned out to be Officer Pritchard, smiled kindly at me and offered his arm, however, I obediently took it, said goodbye to Ward, and allowed myself to be walked home. We passed the investigator from earlier in the day; he doffed his hat to us and continued to Pru's apartment.

"I'll be outside watching the door and windows, Miss," Officer Pritchard said reassuringly outside my door after he searched my apartment. "Not to worry. You just go inside and get some sleep now."

I thanked him and closed the door, locking it securely and

removing my hat, gloves, and coat with shaking hands. After I had double and triple-checked the window locks, I undressed and took myself to bed. I did not anticipate sleep, but somehow my body knew what I needed, and I descended into dreamland almost as soon as my head touched the pillow.

11

When I woke the next morning, I could not remember my dreams, but I was left with a pounding heart and a headache that methodically knocked at my temples as I tried to force down some breakfast but only succeeded in drinking some lukewarm tea. The headache peaked when I got a message from Gene saying Mac needed us at the office.

My headache did not ease until I left my apartment and set out for the *Journal*. I passed Officer Pritchard and waved. He cheerfully returned the wave, followed discreetly until I entered the *Journal*, and then walked by, most likely heading home for a good nap. I wished him beautiful sleep in return for the safe rest he had given me that night.

As soon as I got to my desk, I was accosted by another reporter who pointed to the ceiling and told me with some agitation that Mac had demanded to see me as soon as I arrived. I massaged my temple and ascended the stairs.

Mac's door stood open, and I saw Gene already inside, standing by the desk. He was gazing at a piece of paper in his hands. Mac was puffing determinedly at a cigar and looking out the window. When I closed the door behind me, he turned and gestured to me with the cigar.

"There you are. Look what was delivered here this morning, addressed to you." An odd mixture of dread and curiosity filled me like the sickly smell of the cigar smoke. Gene handed me the paper, looking grim.

> *"Five little dancers met their fate*
> *Five little dancers in sad estate*
> *Five little dancers got their due*
> *Just five little dancers, shame on you.*
> *Murdered 5-4-3-2-1,*
> *Tell the police, 'And then there were none.'"*

It was signed, "the Flower Trimmer."

Revulsion washed over me, and then hatred took its place.

"Foul," I spat, flinging it on Mac's desk.

"And great for today's paper," he said, chewing on his cigar. "Add it in. I'm going to get it photographed, put it in the article, see if anyone recognizes the handwriting." He rubbed his hands together, then removed his cigar and pointed it at me. "If those cops can't net the bird, maybe we can help them out — and make great sales. Get out there and give me your best work." I stared at him until Gene took my hand.

"Come on, Gin," he muttered and pulled me out the door.

I wrenched my arm from his grip and clattered down the stairs.

We sat at the desk, facing each other. Gene put his head in his hands.

"I want him to die," I said through gritted teeth.

"Mac or the murderer?"

"The murderer!"

"So you're sure it's a man now?" Gene looked up and smiled bleakly. "You can't let it get to you, Gin."

I turned on him in disbelief. "You're telling me that this isn't getting to you?"

"I didn't say that." He put his head in his hands again. "It's awful. But we still gotta write the story, Gin. It's our job."

"Did Mac tell the police about the note?"

He shook his head. "I don't know. He'd just shown it to me when you walked in."

I whipped my morsie out of my pocket and tapped with such aggression that the metal stung my finger.

"It's over though now, right?" Gene said, trying to smile and failing miserably. "Just five little dancers' 'and then there were none'?"

I didn't answer. After sending the message to Ward, I was remembering our last conversation, about how he wanted me to send a message to Pru's morsie. The uncertainty about my friend's plight and the horror of the Blaster case had my stomach in knots.

"I went to Pru's apartment last night," I told Gene.

He sat back in his chair. "Did you? To talk to her about the case? What did she say?"

"She wasn't there. I don't think she's been there for a while."

"What do you mean? She's out of town?"

"No." I swallowed. "I mean, I think something happened to her. I brought Ward there, and we saw someone run down her fire escape. They got away."

"What?"

"But Gene…" I leaned forward. "Gene… I sent her a message, and her reply said she was home — as I was standing in her living room, and she wasn't there. Do you understand?"

He raked a trembling hand through his hair. "Gin… what do you think is going on?"

I sat back. "I think something happened to her. I think…" My mind raced. "Maybe she dug up something on her new hunt and someone didn't like it. I'm so afraid… I'm so afraid she's…" I couldn't say it. Gene seemed to understand what I hadn't put into words. He came around the desk and pulled me into his arms.

"It's ok," he said. "It's going to be ok. We'll find her, I promise. There's got to be an explanation."

I fiercely blinked back my tears. Knowing that people around the office could see us, I gently extricated myself. "When was the last time you heard from her? You've been speaking with her about the case?"

He sat down and drummed his fingers on the desk, thinking. "I saw her yesterday after my midday appointment," he said slowly. "She wanted to borrow an autophone for her new hunt. She said something about an affair and corruption, I think. She seemed, I don't know, agitated, scared. We talked about this case, but she was really jumpy. Just before I left, she said something about leaving town for a while. I couldn't get anything else out of her."

I nodded. A tiny pinprick of hope was lighting in my chest. Remembering the blood on the rag, I smothered the light.

"But she seemed eager to talk with you about this Blaster story," he said. "I figured you two would talk this weekend. She said she covered a serial murder once before. But I don't know… she had suitcases by the door. It looked like she was going to leave after I did."

There hadn't been suitcases by the door when we got there; perhaps she'd already left. The smothered hope grew a smidgeon brighter.

"So when did she lose her morsie?"

"You know Pru," he said with a sigh. "She'd lose her head if it weren't attached to her neck. Probably on the train."

"But why would someone answer my messages last night? Like they were her?" I sat back in my chair, my mind whirling.

He had no answer for that.

There was only one thing to do until Ward gave me the message he wanted me to send.

"Time to write," I told Gene as I pulled the cover off my typewriter.

A couple hours passed while Gene and I put pieces of the story together and readied it for Mac and tonight's press. Just before noon, my morsie printed a message from Ward: <QUERY LUNCH STOP WHERE STOP>.

<AT THE JOURNAL WITH GENE STOP> I tapped back. <CAN YOU BRING SANDWICHES STOP>

"Detective Ward is coming," I told Gene. "Maybe he has news on the murders… or maybe something for me about Pru."

"Yeah," Gene sighed, rubbing tired eyes. "We could use some good news."

Ward arrived not long after, bearing four sandwiches, all different kinds. I selected ham and pulled out my small purse as Gene mirrored me with his wallet, but Ward waved both away.

"I got your message about the note," he told me, taking a bite of his salami. "Did you ever play that game?"

"Which game?"

"The counting-down game — quoted on the murder note," he said. "'And then there were none'?"

"No," I said as Gene also shook his head, "I don't recognize it."

"Ah." Ward chewed thoughtfully.

"What do you suppose it means?" Gene asked, picking pastrami out of his teeth.

Ward stared out the window at a small group of children jumping rope on the street. "One could assume that the murderer wishes us to believe that the killing spree is over, perhaps to lessen our guard. Or, on the other hand, it could be a hint that the killer is only halfway through. There are ten deaths in the original song, and we've only discovered five. Whatever the intention, I'm much more interested in pursuing more practical leads. What type of paper? What type of ink?

What type of person has access to these materials? What type of person knows this rhyme? That sort of thing."

I didn't comment; I was busy taking notes.

"A game about death: I understand now why I didn't know it. My mother was rather strict about that sort of thing," Gene said regretfully.

"Will you let me know when you get the report?" I asked Ward.

"Naturally, Miss Harper."

"And do you have a message for me to send?"

He wiped his mouth. "I'd like to talk about that."

"Oh!" I interrupted as I remembered. "Gene told me this morning that he spoke to Pru yesterday. She looked like she was going out of town: she had suitcases by the door."

"And there weren't any when we arrived," Ward said. "Yes. Interesting."

Gene elaborated on what I'd said, telling Ward what he'd already told me. As he spoke, I let my eyes wander around the pressroom, noting the sidelong glances and openly curious looks shooting our way. I couldn't remember another time a policeman had voluntarily walked into the *Franklin Journal*. If I weren't so worried about Pru, I'd be relishing the moment for the history books.

Detective Ward, however, looked like he was right at home as he folded his sandwich paper wrapping into a small, neat square. "Miss Bailey didn't tell you any details about the story she was pursuing?"

Gene shook his head and threw away his crumpled paper. "Nothing but what I told you. She did seem in a hurry — quite upset."

"So we can assume that either she left town and lost her morsie on the way or that someone found her before we did and—" He looked at me. "And she is in trouble."

"I know she might be dead," I heard myself say in a voice that didn't quaver, though my heart pounded painfully.

Ward turned to Gene. "Did she say anything about the previous story she was working on? Anything to indicate that something in the past was troubling her?"

"Nah. She's not working on that one anymore." Gene shrugged. "She told me a couple of days ago that it didn't pan out. As for her past ones, who knows? She's dug up a lot of dirt on a lot of people."

"Miss Harper, would she contact you if she were to leave town?"

I sighed. "I would hope so, but honestly, Pru is very sporadic. She gets very focused on a hunt and sometimes won't talk to me until she's done. But if she were in trouble... I hope she would find a way to contact me if she had to leave town." My mind was whirling. It bothered me that Pru would just drop the story on Milly, especially now that Milly had died. Wouldn't that be the sort of story that Pru would normally sink her teeth into? She must have found something really scandalous to abandon Milly's mysterious gent — and murder.

Ward nodded slowly, still concentrating on Pru's morsie. "I don't know that we can use a message to her to draw this thief out. He will avoid meeting you as he did last night unless... Why he wants you to think he's Pru is troubling to me."

"You think this person is targeting Ginnie?" asked Gene, wrinkling his brow.

Ward considered him. "That is one possibility. I'd advise you to be extra wary, Miss Harper."

"Of course," I said, my head bent over my notes. "Do you have any news on the murder cases?"

"Actually, yes." Ward clasped his hands on the desk and leaned forward. "We found something." He waited as I turned on the autophone and programmed our three voices, and then he continued. "In the alley by the Lily Bed, we found a small metal component. We missed it at first, but on our second sweep, we saw it by the street. There were no fingerprints. It has a manufacturer's name on it — a manufacturer that is used by two factories in town: Panrose Electric, and Vangees Appliances."

I caught my breath sharply.

Gene shook his head.

"I already questioned Mr. Panrose," Ward said. "We found nothing there. I thought I'd see if you two wanted to join me for the Vangees interview since you're working today."

I switched off the autophone and jumped up.

"Finish your sandwich, Gin," Gene said with a small snort.

"I'll bring it." I swept the remains into my pocket. "Let's go."

Shrugging, Gene hefted his bag onto his shoulder and led the way out. Behind me, Ward offered the last sandwich to Mac's harassed-looking secretary, who beamed as she accepted it.

"Do either of you know the Vangees?" Ward asked on our way. I shook my head, and Gene waited until we passed a hoard of shrieking children playing tag before he answered.

"In a roundabout way," he said. "I met them once or twice when I was younger. They're Park people. Been around since before my family and Morislav came to town."

"I see."

The hope of a solid clue and the blue of the sky after a week of intermittent rain cheered me. I unbuttoned my coat and lifted my face to the warm sun rays.

"'Scuse me, Miss!"

The small pick-pocket and his ever-present dog bumped my side and scampered past me, but he wasn't fast enough for my quick eyes or Ward's quicker reflexes.

"Not so fast, Diggory," he remonstrated. "Give the lady back her purse."

I held out my hand, and he returned it, his dog slinking behind him, looking just as sheepish as his owner. Diggory turned to go, but Ward's hand was still clamped on his collar. "And the gentleman's."

His dirty face fell, and he drew out Gene's wallet. The mongrel whined.

Gene swore, but I couldn't help but grin. The talent on this street was applause-worthy.

"Are you still working for Lackwit?" Ward asked, releasing him and holding out his hand to the dog.

"Nah," Diggory kicked a stone down the street. "He got bopped by some bruno. I'm on my own now."

I'd already removed a coin from my purse, but at this I discreetly took out another. "Here," I offered as Ward scratched the dog's back. "And if you're hungry, I've got a half a sandwich."

"Fortunate with your mark today," Ward said to him, rising and clapping him on the shoulder as the boy nabbed the sandwich and money. "Get that sister of yours some milk. Stay away from those crime bosses, you hear? And no more stealing!"

His dog on his heels, Diggory ran before his newfound wealth could be withdrawn.

"I hadn't heard that old Lackwit died," Gene said as we resumed walking.

Ward frowned. "Yes."

"Does that mean Feltz is the only boss left on this side?" I asked, racking my brain for the other names I'd heard whispered with dread in my neighborhood.

"That we know of," answered Ward. "That's what concerns me. Two competing bosses dead this year now."

"You'd think that would be good for your business," Gene said, dodging an overflowing trash can.

"Where do their underlings go?" said Ward. "Is it worse to have several bosses fighting themselves as much as us — or to have one powerful boss who can concentrate only on defeating the law?"

"I see your point," Gene grimaced. "Shall we hope for another villain to take his place?"

Ward harrumphed.

I scribbled a note for a later story. The antics of crime bosses on this side of the city made for normal articles, but a central crime power rising was something Mac would appreciate as front-page news — and something the public should know for their own safety.

The Vangees company comprised a large warehouse on the west side of town with a central office nearby. The office was where we were headed. It was an imposing brick building, well-kept and orderly. The bustling secretaries and salesmen were dressed fashionably, and telephones rang merrily as we entered. When Ward asked to speak to Mr. Vangees Sr., his receptionist showed us straight into his office at the back.

"Coffee, Sonya," he told her as she left. "Sit down, gentlemen, miss. How can I be of service to you today?"

"Could you identify this component for us?" Ward produced the little metal piece from his vest pocket and handed it to Mr. Vangees.

"Certainly," he said, rather taken aback. "It looks like the casing to something," he said after studying it for a moment. "May I ask why you've brought it here?"

"Do you use these specific casings in your processing?"

"Yes, I believe so. I could bring in someone more knowledgeable about the factory work. I concentrate on running the business." He graced us with a patient smile.

"But you do use this manufacturer, correct?"

He squinted at the name inscribed on the metal. "Yes, we use several of their components."

"Are you manufacturing any weapons in your factory?"

He frowned. "What is the real nature of your visit, Officer? And are you recording this interview, Miss?"

"I can just take notes if you prefer," I said demurely.

"What is going on?" he said, his tone becoming snappish.

"We found this piece at the Lily Bed, where a woman was murdered recently," Ward answered, unruffled. "Naturally, I'm following where the evidence leads. This is the second place it has led us. Do you manufacture weapons in your factory, sir?"

"No!" He reconsidered. "Well, yes, on a small scale. You, Officer, are probably carrying a Vangees Stunner on your person."

"True," Ward said.

Vangees' receptionist entered then with coffee. Vangees was peevishly silent as she passed out the cups and didn't speak again until she left.

"Are you suggesting that my company has something to do with these grotesque killings?"

"Not at all," Ward said comfortably, sipping his coffee. "I'm not suggesting anything. I'm simply gathering facts."

"The fact is that we are an honest business doing honest work," said Vangees. "If you think your murderer is using something of ours, that's his business. We have nothing to do with it."

"How would he get his hands on something manufactured here?"

Vangees scowled. "We sell directly to other companies or to the government. An individual could not walk into a store and buy one of our products. It would have to be someone who had been issued our product, or…" he stopped and looked genuinely thoughtful for the first time. "Or he could have stolen it."

"You have something specific in mind," said Ward, watching him. "Did you have a recent burglary?"

"Yes. In fact, we did. A few nights ago. The night watchman saw someone in dark clothing jump from one of our factory windows and run. He was unable to catch the person. We couldn't find anything noticeably out of place or vandalized, but we cannot be sure nothing was missing. We assume that the intent was burglary, since none of our paperwork is stored there and nothing was destroyed."

"Did you report the incident?" asked Ward, taking notes. "When was this?"

Vangees shook his head. "We could find nothing amiss, and our watchman has been known in the past to… er… drink on the job. So we let it go. I believe it was Thursday night, but I am uncertain."

"Could he identify the person if he saw him again?"

"You'd have to ask," Vangees said. "I don't think he got a good look. It was very dark — we don't have many street lights over there."

"I'd like a list of the other products you manufacture that would use this specific casing," Ward said. "Perhaps you can direct me to someone who could assist me."

"Of course," Vangees said, suddenly helpful. "Right this way."

He took us to the engineering department and left after quick introductions. I had the feeling he was glad to be rid of us. While Ward talked to the lead engineer, Gene and I perused the drawings on the wall depicting different products invented by the company engineers.

"Do you know any of these gadgets?" I whispered.

"A few," Gene said in a low voice. "Like he said, they're mostly used for government or commercial use, not sold privately."

"What about the black market?"

"A very real possibility," he conceded. "Ward would do well to do some digging there."

How much digging would have to be done before we unearthed this killer? I wondered wistfully. How deeply was he hidden?

Looking back at Gene, I screwed up my courage. We'd find him. We must. I just hoped it would be sooner rather than later — before someone else was blasted into anonymity.

12

When Ward was finished, he thanked the engineer and returned to us. Noticing the time, we stopped for dinner and then began the walk across town to the area where Gene and I lived.

Itching to be helpful or at least productive, I suggested a brainstorm session and programmed our voices for the autophone to record our thought process.

Gene was of the opinion that the murderer was finished, which meant we now had the advantage of finding him at our leisure.

"With what he said in the note, I bet he had some sort of grudge that he fulfilled. Maybe he had something against the dance houses, wanted to bring them down, scare off the dancers. He got one from each house in town, right?"

Ward nodded. "I've wondered the same thing. However, we can't assume he won't strike again. It's not safe to have him loose in the city. We need to catch him soon."

I shuddered. "Yes. He needs to pay for what he's done."

"There is something that has bothered me for quite some time." Ward focused his piercing gaze on me. "Your friend,

Miss Bailey, is missing, and we know she was pursuing a story about the second murdered woman."

"Coincidence?" suggested Gene.

"He doesn't believe in coincidences," I said, just as Ward said, "No such thing."

I rolled my eyes. "You won't find an ally in that idea, Gene; sorry. It *is* odd that Milly was killed right after Prudence started her story."

"I don't know," he said. "Wrong place, wrong time… a murderer targeting dancers… Milly was out alone… They were all alone, and how common is that for a dancer after hours? Add to that she wasn't the first one murdered, and it looks very doubtful that they had anything to do with each other."

We pondered some more as Luxity began to live up to its name. The fizz and pop of lampposts that were nearing the end of their life punctuated our silence.

"What if, though?" I said slowly. "What if they *are* connected? What if Prudence found something, found this gentleman called Randall, as she said, and what if he had to hush it up?"

"Why kill all those dancers?" said Gene, waving a dismissive hand. "That's far too much work to silence one woman."

"Not if he wanted it to seem like a serial murder instead of an intentional one," said Ward.

"I've wondered, too," I said, "If it could be a copycat: someone killed Ludisia and Milly, and someone else took the idea and killed more dancers."

Ward nodded. "It's frequently entered my mind as well. That is why I investigated the man who stalked the first victim. He has an alibi that is undeniable."

"Maybe he paid someone?" suggested Gene. "To do the dirty deed in his stead?"

Ward shrugged. "It's possible, but his financial records

don't suggest that. He's fallen on hard times. I don't think he had the capital to manage it."

"So we know there was a break-in at the Vangees, and a weapon could have been stolen. Could any of their weapons do that damage?"

"No." Ward shook his head. "I spoke to the engineer about that."

"The break-in could also be for a completely different reason," Gene said. "Electrical parts are expensive. I know you don't like coincidences, but how are we to know that it was related to the murders?"

"I still find it an interesting lead," Ward said, eying him. "Though it seems to have happened between the murders."

"Maybe the murderer needed a replacement for his weapon," I suggested. "If he modified the weapon from the Vangees factory himself, then he might have needed to replace a part."

"Very possible," Ward agreed.

"So." I took a deep breath and ticked off the events on my fingers. "Ludisia is murdered. Milly is murdered. Someone breaks in to the Vangees' factory and escapes out the window. Another three dancers are killed. Pru's morsie is likely stolen, and a person jumps out her window and runs away. We find a blood-filled rag and smoking papers. Pru is missing. And a note is sent to the *Journal* with that vulgar poem."

"It's a unique succession of events." Ward doffed his hat to a patrolman as we passed. The streets were getting darker. "I find the possibility that they could be connected interesting, especially since the person in her apartment was burning papers, which could have been her notes on Miss Smith's story."

"Maybe we need to follow that trail," I said as a lamppost lit up for the night. "And somehow, I've got to contact her. Find out what's going on… if she's still alive."

"You know what I worry about?" Gene said suddenly,

staring up at the stars that shone brightly enough to penetrate the glowing city atmosphere.

"What?" I asked, still feeling the excitement — and dread — of a possible break-through.

He looked at me, and the worry in his eyes touched my heart.

"Gene…"

"You're too close to this now, Gin," he said. "I really am worried that something is going to happen to you if you keep going to interviews with Ward here. No offense," he said.

"I understand," Ward said.

"You're too closely tied to this case. Your name is on the story, the thief who has Pru's morsie is still sending you messages, and whoever jumped out her window probably saw you the other night and knows you're on his tail. Even though they're probably two different cases, it's scary thinking that you're recognized and known to be on the cases by two different, very dangerous people."

"I'm careful, Gene," I said gently. "I've been on dangerous stories before."

"None like this," he argued, stepping around a sleeping mongrel. "None where you've followed a detective around like a puppy dog."

My hackles rose. "I *knew* Milly, Gene. And Pru is missing. This is personal to me."

"That makes it *more* dangerous," he said, shoving his hands into his pockets.

"And it also means I can be an asset," I insisted. "We need to find these people, Gene. What happens to me doesn't matter as much as stopping them from harming people and finding out the truth!"

"And what if they hurt you?" he said, his voice cracking. "You really think that doesn't matter?"

I remembered the overwhelming fear I'd felt in Pru's apartment, the way I had run to Ward at the diner as if someone were chasing me with a blaster. The images of the dead women flashed in my mind, their faces erased forever, their families bereaved, Milly's son orphaned.

I squared my shoulders.

"No. Not if we can stop them from killing people. I'd give my life for that."

I looked away from Gene's exasperated, defeated look and caught Ward staring at me with unshuttered eyes.

"You still think I'm crazy," I said, gesturing to his face.

He shook his head slowly. "I think for the first time I understand you."

My face warmed.

"*I* think you're crazy," Gene said. "And I genuinely wish you'd reconsider. I wish we could drop this nutty case altogether. Too many people have died."

"That I agree with," Ward said as he led us across the street with purposeful steps.

"And that's why we have to pursue it until we find them," I added emphatically, jogging to keep up.

Gene shook his head. "Well, agree to disagree. This is me." He pointed to his apartment. "You'll walk her home, Officer?"

Ward nodded.

Impulsively, I reached out and squeezed Gene's hand. "Thank you," I said.

"For what?"

I stepped back and covered a yawn. "For caring what happens to me."

He shook his head. "Good night, Gin."

"Good night."

He waved to Ward and headed inside.

I turned to go, but Ward looked thoughtfully after him. "How long have you worked together?"

"Five years," I said. "He's a good friend." I felt compelled to explain as we headed for my apartment building. "We both came from society families, so I suppose it bonded us. We've worked well together."

"You've never had a romantic involvement?"

I blushed. "No. He's engaged, remember?"

"Only recently," he said. He saw my red face. "That was rude of me, Miss Harper. I apologize. I have an inquiring mind and a blunt tongue."

"No need to apologize," I laughed a little, trying to wave away my flush. "It's a natural question, I suppose, and an inquiring mind is helpful in your line of work — and in mine. I'm embarrassed too easily: I have many society airs about me still."

"They become you," he said with a slight bow.

"No compliments, please," I begged. "I'm mortified enough."

"I will desist, as you prefer," he said. "Would you take my arm? The construction and lack of lights on this street can make it dangerous at night. The alley to our left is also —"

This is where the second act of my nightmare reared its dark head.

Hearing rapid footsteps behind us, I half-turned as a male figure reached out with a gloved hand that crackled and sparked.

13

I screamed and jolted sideways, barely keeping my feet, as Ward shoved me out of danger and dodged the glove, which left a line of blue electric light where his head had been a second before he dodged. Carried forward by his momentum, our masked attacker fell forward and out of reach between several trash cans that had been left by the street. My heart racing, I looked at Ward, who was clearly doing a very rapid risk assessment. His piercing eyes took in the entire scene in a split second and then met mine with a decision.

"Come!" He took my hand and sprinted down the alley to our left, away from the construction holes and the refuse, which was already emitting sounds of extrication. I let myself be led and glanced to our sides as we went, looking for other threats.

"Can't you shoot him?" I gasped.

"I only have three shots, and we don't know how far that weapon can reach. Let's get you to safety before I turn around to face him." He pulled a silver whistle from underneath his shirt and gave two sharp blasts. "How far can you run in those shoes?"

"Far enough," I said, controlling my breathing for an extended run.

"Watch out," he said, and as we passed more cans, he yanked them to fall behind us, obstructing the path of our would-be pursuer.

I allowed myself a quick look behind as we turned the corner toward some lights in the distance. The attacker was indeed chasing us — without even a limp. I felt Ward's favorite curse word work its way into my mouth, but saved my breath for running instead. Pulling my hand from his, I pumped my arms and lengthened my strides as I'd learned to do as a child playing tag in a very safe, green backyard, hedged in by tall, ornate iron gates.

The light location to which we fled for sanctuary turned out to be another construction site, hosting no people at all and worse, completely blocking our path.

Ward cursed, seeing our pursuer quickly gaining on us, and surveyed the fenced area and deserted surroundings as he blew into his whistle again.

"There," I said, catching my breath and pointing. On the other side of the walled construction, I saw a warehouse that I knew faced a major street by the river that also housed a few restaurants that would be open and bustling at this time of evening. But we had to get over the wall, and the crackling danger was only moments away.

"Can you walk that beam?" Ward asked, glancing behind us. He fired a shot into the dark. From the metallic sound that followed, it must have hit a trash can in the alley. Our pursuer paused and disappeared into the shadows for a moment.

I looked at the I-beam that lay over the wall creating a bridge between the half-constructed building and the warehouse.

Making my decision, I clenched my teeth and ran towards it. He followed. Pounding footsteps could again be heard behind us. As we drew closer, I realized how far we would have to climb to reach the beam.

"Elevator," Ward said, pushing me toward it. It was barely constructed, left open to the elements, simply a way for workers to rise to the most recently built floor. I stumbled into it, scraping my shoulder on the metal frame. Ward firmly closed the gate that made up its door behind us and looked around for the mechanism that would lift us to the beam. I scanned the little box, too, and we saw it at the same time. Remembering a story that Gene and I had covered once that took place on a construction site, I took hold of the lever and pulled, unlocking the mechanism that kept it in place. Up we ascended, but below us our attacker was searching. My heart fell. He'd found another lift on the other side of the building.

"Hurry," I whispered to the elevator, pulling as hard as I could on the lever. It rose at its own pace, unruffled by our urgency, making screeching metallic noises as it passed each steel joist.

"Now," Ward said, already unlocking the gate. I pushed the lever back into its resting position and locked it, then followed him out the door onto the third floor.

A biting breeze rose from the river and set my teeth to chattering, though that could also have been the fear that was beginning to consume me. I concentrated on following Ward step by step across the partially finished floor.

"Almost there," I whispered to myself, endeavoring to ignore the wind. The glare from the lights below partially blinded me when I looked up again to find the beam that was our goal.

I gasped as my foot slipped, and I spiraled my arms to no avail, instead landing hard, straddling a beam just yards from the I-beam and almost slipping off before I righted myself. Ward turned back and leaned down to take hold of my arms and pull me up.

I gasped again and pointed. Our attacker was running

along the edge of the building from the back. Ward yanked me to my feet, and I grabbed his arm for balance as we watched the figure give the I-beam a great shove, and then another. It fell with a mighty boom and crashed down on the other side of the wall.

We turned and began to run back to the elevator.

"Stop!" growled a masculine voice. My heart jumped into my mouth. I felt an urgent hand pushing me forward and looked behind me to see our attacker grab Ward around the head with one hand. They wrestled, the attacker obviously trying to take Ward by his face with the crackling glove. Ward slammed his fist into the man's thigh and then pushed him off; I yelped as Ward's gun shook loose in the tussle and spiraled into the darkness below. His assailant grunted in pain, grabbing his leg.

I saw the Stunner flash in Ward's hand, and then a line of electric current shot toward our attacker, who held up his other hand in self-defense. I watched in disbelief as Ward, instead his assailant, seized up and fell across the metal beam. Lunging forward, I grabbed desperately for his arm as his rigid body tilted crazily toward the floor, two stories down. Just as I took hold of his coat, the dark figure kicked me, and I lost my grip as I was slammed backwards onto the metal beam.

"No!" I screamed as Ward fell, crashing through the partial floor on the story below us and then tumbling out of sight.

Aghast and martialled into fury, I clambered to my feet, pulling my knife from my boot as I rose. Without hesitating or looking down, I ran back to the edge, looking for any other way across. There was none. Hearing my attacker on my heels, I sprinted along the edge. Anger gave me momentum, and I felt that it was possible to outrun him to the elevator if I kept my wits about me. Then, on the other side of the building, I saw a quicker way down. A wooden scaffolding was attached to the side, and it was close enough to the wall to reach. Without a second thought, I put my knife in my mouth (like a pirate, I thought hysterically) and jumped onto the wooden structure. Cursing my skirt as I ran across the scaffolding, I vowed that if I were still alive after tonight, I'd switch to slacks like Prudence.

I heard a bang when my pursuer landed on the scaffolding as well, but I didn't dare waste time in looking back. I'd had enough of a head start that I was almost sure I could climb down to reach the wall first.

The scaffolding trembled, and I doubted myself, but I reached the bottom of the second story safely and braced myself, breathing heavily.

Here goes nothing, I thought, and jumped the remaining distance to the wall.

My hands scrabbled for purchase — and then I grabbed the wooden planks and hauled myself on top, my biceps burning. Again, my skirts hindered my progress, but I swung my leg up and climbed onto the top, hearing the rip of fabric as I went. The fence heaved as the man jumped, too, and with barely a hope, I rolled over the planks, hung from the top for just a moment, and then dropped to the ground.

Thank God, I thought as I hit the ground without breaking anything and then rolled with abandon, skirts tumbling crazily around me. I took my knife from my mouth and pulled myself up to face the masked figure.

He had jumped too, and was standing, facing me.

The electric current sizzled hypnotically between his fingers. Milly's burned body flashed before my eyes, and my courage deserted me. I took to my heels and ran. Music wafted on the wind, coming from the seedy restaurant up ahead. I passed the warehouse and squeezed through the tiny alley that separated it from the adjacent building. On the street now, I ran to the end, where a neon sign lit hope in my agonizingly tired limbs.

As soon as the hope struck me, something else did too. I

tried to scream, but a hand covered my mouth. Out of the corner of my eye, I saw the man's head turning, obviously looking for something. Witnesses, I thought desperately, please let there be witnesses!

I saw nothing but a deserted river and a shaggy dog on a stoop as I struggled for my life. Then even the dog turned tail and slunk into an alley out of sight.

The realization that I was truly on my own infused me with a desperate strength.

I bit down hard, and the villain struck me, making my head reel. His other hand clenched my knife hand. I struggled to free myself as he hauled me toward the river, away from the lights and music that were my only hope. Screaming wildly, I fought with all the energy that remained to me, anticipating the electric current that would render me faceless, just a dead woman discovered by the water. As we reached the dock, I finally found an opening and swung my elbow into it, freeing myself as he jerked back in pain. Breathless, I stumbled backward, putting him between me and the river.

Like lightning, I aimed and flung my blade at him as Pru had taught me. He stumbled backwards, hand raised in defense. Barely deflected by a large ring on his finger, the knife struck his shoulder, and he stepped back, shouting in pain. The next moment, he was rushing toward me, the gloved hand raised. Weaponless, I shrieked for help, turned to run, and was almost bowled over as a street urchin and the shaggy dog raced past me, yelling and barking. I reached out to stop the boy, horrified, and realized that it was Diggory. Before I could register what was happening, his dog had leapt past me, snarling, and I saw the masked murderer flail. When he stepped back, his foot met only air, and he plunged into the water. The dog went with him.

I gasped, but Diggory whistled, and his faithful hound swam back, scrambling up to safety. My heart pounded as my eyes searched the water, but I saw nothing. Feeling as though I were being hunted, despite my narrow escape, I took Diggory's hand and bolted for the restaurant.

The next hour is hazy in my mind. Adrenaline has erased much of the details of what I said, what I did, how the clientele in the restaurant responded — though I recollect quite a lot of shouting.

What I really remember next is leaning over Ward's broken body, calling his name, afraid to face what I was terrified might be true.

14

B ut it wasn't true; he wasn't dead.

"Oh good," he grated out through teeth clenched in pain. "He didn't get you."

Then he promptly lost consciousness.

After we loaded him into the wagon, I noticed the awful way that his leg was bent, and I had to stop myself from vomiting. People looked up at the broken boards above us and at the pile of sawdust where he'd landed (right next to his fallen gun) and whispered about Providence and internal bleeding.

I was just glad he was alive.

At the hospital, I paced the floor of the waiting room after they took him back on a stretcher to assess his injuries. Officer Pritchard and the chief of police were there. It was a rather awkward situation, as Chief Morton was notorious for brushing aside my questions and snarling at the sight of the press anywhere near him. Hearing that Ward had been with me when he fell didn't seem to have endeared me to his superior. However, the chief was able to be professional, if very curt, and told me he'd let me know if anything changed in Ward's condition. When I asked, he also reluctantly informed me that they'd found no sign of the man who had attacked us, but they'd posted patrolmen along the riverfront and were questioning people on the street.

When they went back to see Ward before surgery, I restlessly rose and began pacing again. The plain white walls and unfamiliar smells of the hospital filled me with unease.

Catching the annoyed looks of others in the waiting room, I forced myself to sit, trying not to breathe through my nose. I closed my eyes and gripped my ragged skirt with white-knuckled fingers.

Chief Morton reappeared not long after my left hand went numb. I gathered my courage and asked him about Ward's condition.

"He's going to be all right," he said without looking at me as he put on his hat. "He has a few broken ribs, and one of them punctured his lung. No other internal injuries." Without so much as a goodbye, he walked around me and out the door. I turned, feeling lost, and staggered back to my seat where I remained, my mind blank, until I caught sight of Officer Pritchard hurrying toward me.

"You're that Miss Harper from the first murder, aren't you? The newspaper lady? Detective Ward told me to give this to you. He woke up before they set his leg, and the chief gave him the coroner's report — said they got it back earlier than expected." He scratched his head and studied me uncertainly. "The detective read it while they set his leg and then told me to give it to you as he'd promised. Don't lose it, you hear? He said to bring it back to him tomorrow." He handed me a document, gave me a look that said he wasn't convinced of my trustworthiness but would fulfill his duty to the letter, and headed out into the night. I clutched the papers to my chest and sank into my seat against the wall.

When a nervous father-to-be tried to draw me into conversation as he waited for his wife in labor, I excused myself and stepped outside.

My body was feeling the effects of the night. I trembled, though the evening was not overly cold. Remembering the biting wind atop the steel carcass of the construction site, I shivered violently and closed my eyes, but doing so only brought back the memory of Ward falling from the beams. I pressed my hands into my eyes, willing away the awful sight, as well as the fear that his internal damage could not be reversed, despite the hopeful words of the chief.

Desperate for a friend to confide in, I pulled my morsie from my pocket with fumbling hands and sent Gene a message.

<WE WERE ATTACKED STOP BLASTER MURDERER STOP HE GOT AWAY AND WARD IS INJURED STOP WILL YOU COME TO CENTRAL HOSPITAL STOP>

I collapsed onto a bench outside the hospital, utterly spent. Remembering Ward's gift, I pulled out the coroner's report and squinted at it in the dim light. Never having been able to coax such a valuable document from the precinct before, I was unaccustomed to its style and the vocabulary in which it was written, so I puzzled over it for a couple minutes before several details registered in my mind.

The cause of death was by electrocution. That was obvious enough, I thought. However, the damage was not limited to the burned faces: there was evidence of electrical burn inside their bodies as well. Also, two of the victims had dyed hair: Ludisia and the red-haired woman dragged by the drunk from the Lily Bed. Two of the bodies were still unidentified: the aforementioned redhead and the blonde found at Dahlia's Delights. The redhead's time of death was impossible to tell. The others had an estimated date at least, but when the coroner had inspected her body, he'd found that some of her internal organs showed signs of thawing — as if she'd been frozen. Odd, as none of the nights this week had been cold enough to freeze.

Then something else odd caught my eye. The report clearly stated that the tulip tattoo on the redhead was temporary; the coroner had scrubbed it off and inspected the leavings, finding that it was some sort of plant material instead of standard tattoo ink.

Plant material?

Why would she have a temporary tattoo?

The fact that she and another dancer had dyed hair was unsurprising to me, especially as their career depended on their appearance, but the other dancers had permanent, inked tattoos. Which dance house gave temporary tattoos?

The answer was none. None of them did.

So why...

Unless she wasn't a dancer.

My pulse began to race. I checked the report again.

That dancer was a redhead.

Dread filled me, starting in my abdomen and pushing bile to my throat.

No.

But it made too much sense.

The events of the week began filtering through my mind.

Pru's absence at her planned meeting with Milly. The amount of time before she answered my message. Her "avoidance" of me. The fake message. The cleaned kitchen. The intruder. Her large, overly cold refrigerator and heaped food on the counters.

A thawing redheaded corpse.

A henna tattoo.

My mind was reeling with the idea that the evidence I had in front of me suggested that my best friend had been killed days ago, stuffed in her own refrigerator, tattooed as a dancer with her own henna, and was now lying in the morgue. I looked up, dazed, and saw Gene jogging toward me through the streetlight gloom.

I rose, feeling numb. He held out his arm and enclosed me

safely against his chest. I closed my eyes, breathing his unique scent of engine oil and aftershave. Then, as a well-dressed couple walked by, he stepped back to look at me.

"What are you doing out here? Come inside. You're shivering."

"Not from cold." I shook my head, feeling as though reality was leaving me. "Oh, Gene, I'm so glad you're here."

The lights inside assaulted my suddenly misty eyes. Too bewildered to be dignified, I wiped my runny nose and told him everything that had happened after we'd left him. He listened carefully, absently offering me his handkerchief. I was just about to tell him what I'd hypothesized from the coroner's report when a nurse emerged from the back rooms. Seeing me, she walked briskly over to us and told us that Ward's injuries had been tended to and that he was resting upstairs.

"That nice officer told me you'd want to know," she said, smiling at my relieved face.

"Can we see him?" I asked, hardly daring to hope.

"Not tonight." She shook her head. "But do come back in the morning, Miss. Visitors would be good for him. He's in room six-eleven right now."

She gave us another smile and then left.

"I wish we could see him," I whispered, clutching at Gene. "The last I saw him was just… too horrible."

"Let me go," Gene said conspiratorially. "If I get in trouble, then it's me, not you. And if I can see him, I'll be able to tell you how he is."

I breathed a shaky sigh as he walked confidently toward the doors. Noticing that the father-to-be was eying me again, I went back outside to the bench where I'd waited for Gene.

Dreading another wait, I felt around in my pockets and found the autophone. It was still on. Gene would surely scold for that, I thought, but it only held a few hours' worth of audio before it stopped recording, so I should still have the last session. Desperate to escape all that was tormenting my mind,

I played it from the beginning, pulling out my pad of paper and pencil to take notes.

This time *I* was in the top-of-the-fold, front-page story, I thought bitterly. Not my usual way of making a story — and certainly not my preferred method. I wrote quickly, my hands becoming steady and sure as I concentrated on my note-taking instead of the grief rising in my heart.

The brainstorm session with Ward and Gene started playing after the interview with Vangees. With the coroner's report beside me, I found myself certain that the murders and Pru's story about Milly were linked. I tapped my pencil on my thigh, thinking, as I listened absently to my conversation with Ward continuing after we parted ways with Gene. I ignored the autophone as it kept running. The murders had started right after Pru began following Milly's story, and then Pru's disappearance — and probably death — but wait! Gene had seen her just the other night and said she was on a different hunt… I put my head in my hands, pushing away exhaustion as I pondered. Could I be wrong?

I jerked back to the present. On the autophone, I heard Ward's curt words and my breathless voice on top of the construction site. The words were slightly muffled, as the autophone had been in my pocket, but I still shuddered as they brought back the traumatic memories of just a couple of hours before. I reached out to turn off the device when I heard, "Stop!"

My hand recoiled. The voice had come from the autophone, from when we'd faced our attacker on those great metal beams — but the voice coming from this little device was not Ward's or mine.

I remembered running toward the elevator and hearing that voice come from behind us — just before Ward was attacked.

My heart pounded, and it felt like my brain constricted

inside my head. The street in front of me blurred as I realized what it meant.

I had the voice of the blaster murderer, the self-proclaimed "Flower Trimmer," on the recording in front of me.

And the only other voice that I had programmed into the autophone before all that happened was Gene's.

15

A very important fact cut through the shock numbing my brain: Gene was at this moment making his way up to the room where Ward lay helpless.

I felt as if I were mired in molasses as I lurched to my feet and ran.

Through the doorway into the bright room. Through the back doors, past the nurse at the desk who called out to me. Through the hallway, my eyes fixed on the stairs.

He's going to kill Ward.

Somewhere far above me — was I imagining it? — I thought I heard a concussive sound. I pounded up the stairs, floor by floor.

I pulled my skirt above my knees and gasped for breath, taking the stairs two at a time.

He's killing him now.

The sixth floor door was just ahead of me. My lungs burned and my calves protested as I bolted towards it.

A different sort of bang — like thunder — sounded. Three seconds later, another one followed.

I sprinted down the hall, pushing aside people who had stopped at the sound and were looking around in shock.

Searching, searching, scanning the numbers on the doors
— there!

Six-eleven.

I yanked the door open and staggered inside, then realized
I had no weapon, no way to stop Gene from finishing the lead
detective on his case.

But Gene wasn't there.

Instead, Ward was sitting up in bed, his revolver in his
shaking hand.

"He ran," he rasped, his face white with pain. "I clipped
him, but he got away."

I reached for the Stunner on his bedside table, but he
stopped me.

"His ring — deflects the current. Don't go after him alone.
Stay —"

But I was already out the door again.

Why was I running after him?

I didn't know at the time.

I saw a nurse, fallen on the ground, clearly dead,
electrocuted. Farther down, I saw another — also dead. The
body lay blocking the threshold of the door that led to the
roof. I jumped over it, feeling sick, and ran up the stairs,
panting with exhaustion and… something else.

The Hunt.

The Hunt had taken me, just as it had the moment I saw
Nathaniel die, pushed off the grand hall balcony by his father,
his death never recognized for what it was: murder.

I was hunting for truth once more.

It was not fear that caused my limbs to tremble and my
breath to catch as I emerged on the roof of the hospital.

I found what I was looking for in an instant: Gene huddled
by the edge of the roof, cradling his arm. Now I noticed the
awkward way he held his shoulder, the shoulder where my
knife had found a mark and where Ward's bullet had lodged.
When I looked down, I saw blood spotting the dark rooftop.

Lights were on all over Luxity now, but the roof was its own world in this moment, all shadows and dark outlines.

I walked toward him, and he made as if to rise.

"Just stay there," I said in a low voice. "Just stay there and tell me why."

"Then you know," he said hoarsely.

"I don't know the most important part: I don't know *why*. Tell me why, Gene. Why Prudence? Why all those other women? You almost killed Ward — you almost killed me!" The realization shook me to my core. "Tell me why!"

"I would never have killed you, Gin," he pleaded, but as I drew closer, I saw the look in his eyes.

"Yes. You would have. Tell me the truth. Now."

He pulled back, shuffling awkwardly against the floor. "I've got a future!" he spat. "She wouldn't let me have that! It's not my fault! I've got Helen; I've got to advance this city; I've got my work to do! But she wouldn't let me go. 'Got to provide for your son,'" he mimicked in a high voice. "As if I were the only possible father of the brat! She was a whore!"

"Milly." I understood now. "You are Randall, 'the gent with the fern in his hat.'" I remembered Milly's voice recounting the story. "You heard her at the *Journal*, from back in the hallway. You knew she was looking for *you*."

His face was ugly with hate. "Could've been anybody. But she decided on me, and she wouldn't just let it *go*. It wasn't my *fault*."

"Then why all the others?" My voice was quiet, steady. I advanced on him.

"They would have figured it out. It was too obvious." His voice was a wild muttering, as if he were reciting something he'd told himself over and over for the last week. "Had to make it look like a guy with a thing against dancers. I couldn't just stop."

"But Ludisia was first, not Milly. Why her?"

"She wouldn't get out of my way. She saw me, saw my

glove. Knew I was looking for Milly. She should've just let me go. I had no *choice*."

I clenched my teeth. "No choice? Just another lie, Gene. You killed five innocent women. How can you possibly justify that?"

"The connections! They would have traced it to me!"

For the first time, I saw the rabid look in his eyes, and I was afraid.

"Milly and Ludisia! The police would trace them to me! Prudence — she was connected, too." His face constricted; I glimpsed the terror that had driven him to strike down woman after woman. "It was essential… I had to… had to make it look like a guy on a mission to kill a dancer from each house… That was all… just five…"

"Just five?" I stared at him, nauseous. "Gene… what about Prudence? She was our friend!"

"I told her to get off the case! Told her it was dangerous! You saw her! She never could let a story go. She was bound to get herself in trouble someday. Stupid bi—"

"She wasn't," I said. Inexplicably, despite the hatred that knotted my stomach, I felt grief — not just for Prudence, for Milly, for the other women. I was also grieving for Gene, my friend.

"You didn't have to," I said. "Surely you know that. One can always find another way."

"There wasn't another way! You have no idea! You don't care about anything except writing your pointless stories! You have no idea what it's like to be ambitious, to be part of something bigger than yourself!"

I shook my head, the grief rising. "Why didn't I see that your inventions, that getting back into high society, were more important to you than human life?"

"You don't understand," he snapped. The desperation contorted his face. He turned away from me.

"I don't," I said, clenching my fists. "But that doesn't

matter. You have to pay for it now. You have to turn yourself in. You went too far."

He barked out a bitter laugh. "Too far? Changing the world, advancing humanity was too far? *I* matter, Ginnie Harper! Just as much as Yuri Morislav and all the other great men of our century! And I *will not* turn myself in." I was only a stride away when he stood suddenly, one arm hanging, the other hand clenched in a fist. His glove crackled. "You can't stand in my way."

Lights flickered in the city below. Velvety blackness reigned above. I felt completely alone — alone with a killer.

"I will."

"No," he said. "I'm going to leave. I won't kill anyone else. My note was genuine — I'm done."

The ugly memory of the nurses murdered on the floor downstairs still vivid in my mind, I shook my head. Perhaps even *he* didn't realize he was lying. But I knew. He'd never stop, not if he thought someone, anyone, might find out. There was no end to this path he had chosen.

His voice turned sharp. "You're going to let me go, and you will not tell this story. It's finished, Ginnie. Let me go. It's all over."

"I'm sorry," I said, and I was — for him. "But I can't. The truth must be known — for everyone's sakes. And you must make it right."

"You'd die for that? For your truth?" He raised the glove. In the solitary darkness, the crackling light was beautiful. A strange peace filled me.

"Yes."

His eyes were tortured. "Fight me, Gin. Give me a reason."

I let my arms hang slack at my sides. "No. You have no reason to kill me besides your own greed. If you're going to kill me, know that. You have no excuse for the choices you've made to murder your own soul."

His face hardened. He reached out.

I refused to close my eyes, instead looking past the bright light dancing between his fingertips and into the eyes of the man I'd called my friend.

Then his hand withdrew.

Without another word, he turned his back, took hold of the low wall at the edge of the roof, and vaulted over it, abandoning himself to the darkness.

EPILOGUE

My candles are gone. The last has flickered out, and my wrists ache from writing. I pause for a moment now to massage the three black ribbons that encircle my wrist to remember my friends who have gone before me in death.

Telling my story — and that of Gene, Prudence, Nathaniel, Milly, and Ludisia — has brought me one step closer to closure. Though this story has ended, my story continues.

So do Gene's and Milly's, in a way.

After I sent in the final draft of the final story to Mac (he published it without editing a single word), Gene's father came forward. In their sorrow, he and Gene's mother came looking for their grandchild. They provided for little Lawrence, visited him often, and when Milly's mother, his guardian, succumbed to pneumonia not long after, they took him in, gave him their name, and raised him. In my moments of utter darkness, I remember his baby grins and the joy in their faces, and I cling to the hope of new life.

Detective Ward is soon to be back on the job. He will carry a cane for a few months, but his ribs and lung are healing, and his mind is as sharp and his eyes as piercing as ever.

I have no new assistant at the *Journal* yet, nor do I want one. I believe Mac will hire someone eventually, and perhaps by that day, I will have learned to trust again.

For now, I take to the streets, hunting ever to honor the fates of my friends, remembering the choices they made and still marveling that my own choices did not lead to my death.

There must be a reason for that, and so I hunt on.

Ginnie Harper, reporter for the *Franklin Journal.*

THANK YOU!

Thank you for reading the first of Ginnie's stories!

Do you have a minute for feedback? Reviews help readers and authors: more reviews make books more visible so more readers can find them, (which means I get more support and can write more books), and thorough, honest reviews let me know what I'm doing well *or* what I need to improve!

Want to read more Ginnie Harper? Sign up for new book updates on www.britneydehnertbooks.com/ GinnieHarperSignUp! After you've done so, go to www. britneydehnertbooks.com/ginnie-harper-mysteries, and you can find behind-the-scenes goodies like book study questions and printables, the "Why" behind the names of this story, historical references, deleted scenes and more!

BONUS CHAPTERS

Read on for the first two chapters in *Truth in the Water*, the second installment in Ginnie's story.

TRUTH IN THE WATER PROLOGUE AND CHAPTERS 1, 2

Since the Blaster Murders, I have found that writing a personal account of the more troubling stories I cover enables me to process what I have seen, heard, and learned. I have not yet encountered a story that wounded me as the Blaster Murders did, but nonetheless, thoroughly recounting each case and story has given me a certain peace of mind.

The newest story I hunted took me down a very odd and twisted path. I believe I will have some difficulty in transcribing this particular case, but I will endeavor to do so in hopes that I may uncover more of the truth that is still hidden to my mind's eye. Unlike the Blaster Murders, this case is not definitively closed. Though Ward has declared it over, I must admit that I am not completely satisfied, and sometimes when we speak of it, I see in his eyes that he is not either. Perhaps we never will be.

For me, this story started on my way home from the Journal. I had just stopped for a chat with Diggory and his dog, Rufus, sharing the meat pie I'd made the previous night and the apples they'd earned by running errands for the grocer. Rufus appreciated the meat pie, gulping down more than his fair share. A glittering automobile splashed last night's puddle over our lower legs while I Rufus in shocked tones and Diggory laughed at me. Sighing at my drenched stockings, I glanced up to see the woman who stepped out of the automobile, and my jaw dropped in a most unladylike fashion.

"Chas?" I said.

The fashionably bobbed head swiveled in my direction.

"Ginnie? I didn't recognize you!" Her manicured hand rested on her heart.

I scrambled to my feet, brushing crumbs from my trousers. A delivery truck rumbled by, splashing across the curb again. "What are you doing here?"

Rufus stood at attention, eying the newcomer with interest, while Diggory jumped up, his head swiveling between us.

"I… I was looking for you, actually," she stammered. "I had heard that you lived… well, there." She pointed to the apartment building behind us.

"It's good you bumped into me then." I half-smiled. "I live a block from here."

"Oh," she said. Her hand jumped to her pearl necklace.

"Are you headed to a party?"

"After this… errand, yes."

We stood awkwardly for a moment.

Diggory whistled a discordant harmony in that oddly talented way he had, and I jumped a little.

"Pardon me. This is Diggory. And his dog, Rufus, of course." I gestured to the woman. "Diggory, this is my sister, Chastity Jefferson."

"Pleased to make your acquaintance, I'm sure," she said, bending her head delicately.

"Oh me, too," Diggory said with enthusiasm, seizing her hand. "You're a right and proper lady, ain't ya?"

My mouth twitched. "Yes, Diggory, she is. And Diggory is quite the hero, Chas."

Her left eyebrow rose ever so slightly. "Oh?"

"He and Rufus saved my life last February. Perhaps you read about the Blaster Murders?"

She blushed a light pink. "Yes. I read your stories without fail, actually."

I was pleased in spite of myself. "Then you may have read about the murderer's attack on a detective and myself. He was about to finish me off when Rufus and Diggory took him by surprise and chased him into the river."

Diggory swung his arms by his sides. "I dunno as you wouldn'ta got 'im your own self, Miss Harper," he said, modest as any street lad could be. "That little blade was a nice touch."

Chastity blinked at this extraordinary statement and turned to me. "I forget that you go by Harper now. Perhaps you've heard that I am no longer a Jefferson either? Though not by the same means, of course."

"You've married?" I asked, taken aback.

She nodded, and her finely penciled eyebrows contracted. "It wasn't in any of the papers, because he's of new money, and, well, Father was not exactly pleased with me marrying someone from the Hill. He was also dead set against having you there, and…" She looked away from me. "Ginnie, I…"

I waved away her unspoken apology, feeling stung nonetheless. "I understand. Of course. It was my choice to leave, not yours."

"But to treat you like a leper," she said, wrinkling her nose. "Surely that is unnecessary."

I shrugged. "Not to Father, I suppose. But tell me — who is the lucky man?"

Her shoulders squared, the black and silver fabric of her dress shimmering in the noon sun. "Perhaps you remember the Ottisons?"

I nodded. Even poor reporters know the name of the richest steel mogul in the city. He was certainly new money — quite a bit of new money.

"Edwin is the eldest son. We were married last spring."

Diggory whistled through his teeth. I remember thinking the sound was more menacing than impressed, though I had no idea why.

"Congratulations," I said, trying to sound hearty and succeeding only in feeling foolish.

The fringe on the bottom of her dress rustled as she studied my face.

"Perhaps we could speak somewhere…"

"Else?" I finished, remembering my manners. "Of course. Please come up for tea. Diggory, thank you for lunch. The baker promised me a special batch of donuts tomorrow if you'd like to meet me there."

His gossip-hungry face had fallen, but at the sound of such a treat, it lit up again.

"Hot dog! Come on, Rufus! Nice meetin' ya, Miss!"

Rufus gulped the rest of his meat pie, and they raced down the street.

I turned back to my sister, smiling, and saw her dubious expression turn to polite interest.

"Quite an engaging little urchin, isn't he?" she offered.

For just a second, I remembered the heart-pounding moment I knew I would live another day instead of dying at the hands of a serial killer — because of the courageous actions of that "engaging little urchin" and his dog.

I sighed. "Quite. Do you want to drive, or shall we walk? It's not far."

Her gaze took in the fallen refuse in front of the next building, the men in jaunty caps whistling and joking across the street, and the little girl making mud pies in the gutter.

"I should see your neighborhood, of course," she said, holding out her hand. I took it with a hidden smile and tucked it in my arm. She smelled of rose water, which immediately took me back to a room papered in violets where she and I stared at the light winking off cut glass perfume bottles lining Mama's dresser.

"When I'm a lady, I'll always wear rose water," she had declared in her high, childish voice. She was eight.

"You only say that because Lady Eleanor does," I had snipped back, my greater age and experience making me superior.

"And you only say that because you've started French and think you're better than me," she'd returned. "Anyway, rose water is what all the grand ladies wear, and I am going to be a grand lady someday."

"You!" I'd chortled, looking at her little black ringlets and cherub face.

Yet here she was, the closest thing to a grand lady that this city could produce, walking arm in arm with me, a working journalist, through the poor lower city and stepping around horse manure.

I shook my head. Times certainly do change, and often not according to one's expectations.

"This is where I live," I said when we reached my apartment building.

"Why, it looks exactly like the other," she declared. "No wonder Jacques was confused."

We mounted the front steps. "What will your driver do while we're inside?" I asked, looking over my shoulder at the car that had slowly followed us. "Shall I ask him in?"

She made a shocked noise. "He'll be fine in the car. My goodness! What an upside down way you live now. Asking the chauffeur inside!" She shook her perfectly groomed head and laughed.

"I daresay he'll get dreadfully hot, Chas," I said. "You have him in quite the suit."

She waved away my comment as I retrieved my key from

my vest pocket and inserted it, jiggling the handle to help it unlatch.

"He's used to the heat. Ginnie dear, shall I send him to the patisserie for some tea things?"

"Oh, I've got some cookies and even your favorite rose tea," I said. "I don't know why I keep it on hand, to be honest. I never drink it."

"I was meant to visit," she said, smiling at me and removing her gloves as we walked into the shabby three-room apartment.

"Make yourself comfortable," I called, heading to the small corner kitchen to put on the water and take out the cookies from the tin on the counter.

"Is this your parlor?" she said humorously, fixing her hair in the mirror across from the rickety table.

"And dining room, kitchen table, and drawing room," I chuckled. "Sit in the chair with the green cushion. The other has quite the personality, and I'm afraid it doesn't behave for visitors."

"So what do you do with yourself when you're not writing about murder and mayhem?" she asked, sitting gingerly in the correct chair and crossing her ankles.

I measured the tea and checked the hissing water. "Not much, I suppose. I've taken to writing an account of the criminal cases I cover, but I've not much of a social life."

She looked sympathetic. "No men chasing you? Your figure is still to die for. I'm desperately jealous."

I shook my head, smiling. "As self-deprecating as always. You look wonderful, Chas."

"So that's a no?" she probed. "Not a single, dastardly handsome man?"

My lips twitched as I thought about my midweekly chats with Thomas Ward. She'd find a detective's friendship about as compelling as a street urchin's. "I look forward to the day when Diggory becomes such an appealing man. For now, I'll have to pine away until he's old enough, I suppose."

A ladylike sigh escaped her tinted lips. She hesitated before she spoke again. "It's Nathaniel, isn't it?"

My chest tightened as it always did when I thought of him. "No. It's not."

Her brown eyes filled with pity. Anger inexplicably rushed over me.

"It's been a long time, Ginnie. Look at your kid sister if you don't remember how time passes." She put her chin in her hands and looked reflective. "I could bring you along to some parties, you know." Her eyes were measuring me. "Get you a new dress or two, bob that hair, and I'm sure we could land you a husband with a full bank account and a Ford motorcar."

"Not a Rolls Royce?" I asked, raising an eyebrow.

She shrugged and sipped at the tea I handed her. "With your stubbornness, I'm sure you could have gotten back into society by now if you'd really wanted to. I'd settle for a Ford man if it's what you wanted."

I chuckled weakly, knowing she was after a laugh. "I've never been one for parties, if you remember. And honestly, I'd rather walk. Fords and Rolls snag a bit too much attention around my neighborhood."

She sat back with a sigh. "But that's the whole point, dear. You needn't stay in your neighborhood. A man could make your life easier. You needn't give up your writing either," she added, raising a hand as I opened my mouth. "These are modern times. Why, you could publish books, submit to magazines. No need to scrape a living with that newspaper. You'd have more time on your hands with a servant or two." She glanced at my battered piano-miniature on the table. "You could buy a real piano. Don't you miss that?"

I studied her face, feeling protective of my tiny instrument, which I'd played every night since the Blaster Murders: it helped me calm down before bed. Oddly, I'd even taken to tapping out melodies during the day when I was anxious and didn't have it near.

Chastity reached over and poked me. "Ginnie? Yoo-hoo! Don't you miss our Grand piano at home?"

I shrugged and took a bite of cookie, knowing she was getting at something else. "You have someone specific in mind for this daydream life, don't you?"

When she merely sipped her tea in response, I tapped a rhythm on my knee. "When did you pick up matchmaking? It doesn't become you."

"We'll talk of something else," she said, putting her tea down in a conciliatory gesture.

"Yes, let's. Tell me about your husband. Edwin, was it?"

She nodded and pushed the tea away, lines suddenly appearing on her forehead. "Edwin is a lovely man, but I'm worried about him."

"What?" I asked, startled. "Why?"

Her chair creaked. She fiddled with her cookie. "He's ill. And I don't know what's wrong."

"The doctors don't say anything?"

She waved a hand impatiently. "They're useless. One knife-happy quack almost removed his appendix. Another said it was ulcers." She shuddered. "Edwin's temper certainly reared its head with that one. The doctor prescribed milk for his stomach through a tube in his nostril."

My hand covered my nose in a reflexive action. She nodded. "It was ghastly. No, the doctors don't know what's wrong." She leaned forward. "Ginnie, I came to you for help."

"What do you mean?"

"People are saying that it's that new hydroelectric generator outside the city, the one that Panrose Electric built. They're saying that it's causing issues with our drinking water. Edwin's not the first one to get sick. Others on the Hill have the same problems: stomach pain, cramps, vomiting, dizziness... horrid stuff."

I rubbed my forehead. "It sounds like a stomach virus. Why would it be the new generator?"

"Remember Gaines? Owner of Sero Electric?"

I nodded. He lived in the Park, near where we grew up.

"He's saying that it can't be a coincidence. He's calling for them to shut the generator down."

"Then why do you need my help?"

"We need the press. Panrose won't do anything about it. They're ignoring us." She paused. "A friend of mine delivered a stillborn child last week. She's been ill with it, too, even before she got pregnant."

I took a deep breath and let it out slowly. "What do you want me to do? I don't do smear stories."

"I understand. But something is better than nothing. Please, Ginnie." She blinked tears from her eyelashes. "I don't know what I'd do without Edwin."

"I'll talk to Mac," I said, picking up my tea. "But why aren't you sick, if it's the water?"

Chastity sniffed. "You know I drink nothing but pure orange juice and champagne."

I raised my eyebrow again and settled back in my chair. "You're drinking tea right now, Chas."

"I stopped when Edwin wouldn't hear of letting our cook go. She makes abominably bitter tea." She took another sip and wiped her eyes, giving me a small smile. "But her leg of lamb is divine. And her cakes. I must have you over, now that we've reconnected."

My eyes twinkled. "But what would I wear?"

"Your birthday's coming up, isn't it?" she said innocently. "Give me your measurements, that's a dear."

My mind full of our conversation, I went to Mac the next day to do as I'd promised.

"What? What?" he snapped impatiently. "A new story? What about that story on the mayor's affair? Already done? Fine, fine. It's potentially scandalous? On the electric companies?" His eyes gleamed. "Great, great. Go for it. Take Jacks with you."

"Mac, I really think…"

He waved me out as his phone rang insistently. "No thinking, Harper. Take Jacks and go. I've got a call coming — yes! Mac here! What do you want?"

I backed out and closed his door. Mac had taken to thrusting new assistants on me, hoping for someone to stick. I didn't want a new assistant, but my partially articulated protests landed on deaf ears. Jacks was the greenest one yet. He wasn't a photographer or a journalist or even a tinkerer like Gene had been; he was just a former copywriter from one of the lesser advertising firms in Luxity. I sighed as I walked down to find him.

I was relieved — and slightly aggravated — to find that he wasn't in, and I headed to my desk to retrieve an autophone. To my surprise, a young woman met me there.

"Felicity Jacks," she said, sticking out her hand. I took it, speechless.

Felicity Jacks was the most uncommon-looking person I had ever met. Her hair was bright orange, her eyes bright blue. Her freckles took over her face and arms (what I could see of them under her plain brown coat), and her nose was long and thin. But what truly impressed the beholder of this unique personage was the mischievous glint in her azure eyes. They were framed by lashes almost ridiculously long, even brushing the top of her eyebrows, and blackened by makeup. Judging by her milky complexion, I assumed her eyelashes were naturally almost white. The effect of those darting, intelligent, vividly colored eyes with the startling long lashes was one not to be forgotten.

"Hello," I said stupidly.

"You're Ginnie Harper," she supplied for me, smiling coyly. "Mac set me to work with you. He said I'm sixth in a long line since your last assistant kicked the bucket last year."

I winced. "I haven't exactly been counting…"

"Oh, I would if I were you," she said with relish. "It seems such an excellent record. I'm all shivery inside with motivation to do a bang-up job."

"I…" I was at a loss. "I thought Mac had assigned Terry Jacks to me, not… what did you say your name was?"

She threw her head back and laughed. "Terry, Terry. Oh, he'd be hopeless! I'm Felicity, and boy are you lucky you have me instead of him. He's my cousin, you know. And a complete incompetent. He got me this job, but that's the best thing I can say about him. No, Mac assigned me to you as soon as I got hired —" she flicked her wrist upside down to check her watch — "approximately one hour ago." She grinned at me, and my stomach dropped into my shoes. "This is going to be fun."

Searching desperately for something to say, I tried again. "Your gloves are lovely. I've never felt something so soft."

She lifted her hand dramatically to her forehead. "Thanks awfully. I worked in a glove factory two jobs before this. Snatched the best ones before I left — paid for them, don't worry." Her eyes twinkled at my expression. "They're cowhide but softened differently than leather. You don't see them much in the lower city."

"Two jobs before this? Where else have you worked?"

"Oh honey, you lost count of your assistants; I lost count of my jobs. We're even." She furrowed her brow and started ticking names off her fingers. "Let's see. I worked for the telegraph company — can't remember the name now — I worked the switchboards at Morislav's 'Phone Company, I was a secretary at the Vangees Company, a laundress at Nelly's Laundry, and a waitress at Delly's Diner. They sound related, don't they? Nelly and Delly? It's such a scream that I worked at both." She laughed delightedly and adjusted the strap of her bright green purse on her shoulder. "I even cleaned for the nuns at that Catholic school on the east end. That's when I took up photography with my dad's camera. They threw me out after a month, but I had a real time of it."

I found myself spellbound — or perhaps dazed. "You're quite the jack-of-all-trades."

She grinned evilly. "And you like your puns. Mac didn't tell me that."

It took me a moment before I realized what she meant. "Oh. Yes. Felicity Jacks. Sorry. So Mac hired you today then? And assigned you to me?" I was still reeling.

She nodded smugly. "Terry told me his boss was a modern newspaper man who did everything his own way, and I should have believed him. I didn't think he'd hire a woman for anything but a secretary, but he sure did, and I'm just as pleased as punch. So where are we off to first? I've got my camera all ready."

She looked at me expectantly, and it finally sunk in to my stunned brain that this extraordinary woman was in my charge now. I took a deep breath.

"Sero Electric." I rummaged for my autophone and an extra pad of paper, trying to organize my thoughts. Once I was satisfied that I'd gathered myself together sufficiently to explain the investigation, I looked up and found that she had already bounded out the door.

I was staring, my mouth slightly open, when another reporter hurried up with a stack of papers in his arms. He gave an admiring whistle and indicated the door with his head.

"How'd you get the new one, Ginnie? Mac should've given her to someone who would appreciate what he's got. Like me, for instance. I s'pose he thought the ladies should stick together, eh?" He gave a despondent shake of his head and left.

I rolled my eyes and hurried to the door. The first day on this story was already more exciting than I had bargained.

"There you are," Felicity said as I caught up to her. She'd been standing, hands on her hips, facing the street a block down from the Journal. "Sero Electric is this way, isn't it?" She jabbed to her right with her thumb.

I nodded. "We're going to ask them some questions about the new hydro-electric generator by the Hill. My si—an acquaintance gave me the lead."

"A si—quaintance, huh?" she said, eyes sparkling. "I have those, too. Very handy for leads. Will I be photographing anything today? I don't usually carry this just for exercise." She hefted the camera bag.

"We'll see," I said. "We don't often print pictures because it's costly, but I like to have them for reference. Can you develop them as well?"

"Barely. I plan to get better at it here. I met your developer today and decided I could use some time in that dark room with him." She waggled her eyebrows. I gave her a weak laugh, trying unsuccessfully to remember if someone semi-attractive worked in the darkroom. I gave up and went on.

"I'd like to get over to Panrose Electric as well, to get their side of it. This is just the beginning of my investigation."

"Oh, that's swell. I'm so glad I joined up today. I can't wait to see start-to-finish how you do this reporting lark. When Terry told me about this job, I went back and read all the Journals I could find. Your articles were my favorite. I'm just too excited to work for you."

"You're not working for me," I said, blushing. "Mac's your boss. We're just working together, that's all." For now, I added in my mind, thinking of the last five. Obviously, though, Felicity was going to be different. She might be the first assistant to quit after only one day on the job when she saw how boring the beginning of an investigation can be.

She kept up a pretty constant stream of talk all the way to

Sero's, politely remembering me from time to time and asking questions about everything from my childhood friends to my favorite coworkers to the best places to "grab a bite" while on the job. My head was spinning by the time we were ushered into Mr. Gaines' office, but somehow I also couldn't keep a silly grin off my face.

Gaines wiped that grin away immediately. "I'm not buying anything," he snapped. "I'm a very busy man." I instantly thought of the only slightly less hostile Mr. Vangees, whom I'd interviewed in the Blaster Murders. The two shared an uncannily similar inhospitable air.

"We're not here to sell you something, Mr. Gaines," I said patiently, reaching out to shake his hand. "We're here about the hydroelectric generator. I called you last night, remember?"

He frowned. "You said a reporter would be coming, who I assumed would be your boss."

"Actually, I'm the reporter," I said, accepting the reluctant shake he offered me. "My name is Ginnie Harper, and I've written articles for the Franklin Journal for several years now. I'll be conducting the interview. This is my... assistant, Miss Jacks."

His face cleared, but only slightly. Felicity had the wisdom to remain silent. I straightened my vest and sat as he did. Holding the button to program the autophone, I began recording. I'd have to teach Felicity how to handle the autophone later: I really should have taught her on our way here, but I hadn't had the presence of mind to do so.

"I've heard you have some concerns about the generator and its effect on the public's health. Would you be kind enough to tell me about that?"

Gaines cleared his throat. "Yes, of course. When Panrose Electric installed that blasted thing, I knew it was going to be trouble. Morislav has done great things for our city, but some of these new machines are simply dangerous. We've tested the water coming through it, and it's contaminated. Reports of an epidemic amongst the fine citizens of the Hill confirm that the water is not only contaminated, but actually deadly as well! It's a crying shame that Luxity allowed Panrose their way."

"What sorts of tests have you done?" I asked, scribbling short-hand notes.

"Several of the chemical sort that my people would have to explain to you," he said, favoring me with a condescending smile. "I'm sure your schooling wouldn't quite have covered it."

"The schooling of many of our readers should be adequate, though," I answered sweetly. "I try to be as thorough as possible. I'm sure you understand: it's a basic requirement of my profession."

He was trying without success to keep a scowl from taking over his rather jowly features. "Then you can set an appointment with my chemists, Miss Hopper."

"Harper," I smiled. "And thank you. What else leads you to believe that the sickness on the Hill is connected to the generator?"

"I would think it obvious that the only commonality between all these people getting sick is the water that they drink and bathe in," he answered. "Logic tells me that can't be a coincidence. I saw the plans for the generator before they put it in, and I'll tell you now," he jabbed the table with his forefinger, "Panrose has no consideration for safety for their customers. They're only after the money. Follow the money, I always say."

"Quite so, Mr. Gaines," I said, crossing my legs to continue writing on my knee. "What were their reasons for installing a new generator?"

"What else? Attention! If they can get some press over a new-fangled machine, customers will flock to them for the 'modern experience.'" He snorted. "Those poor new money types on the Hill are just the sort to fall for that kind of thing.

Always looking for something new and exciting." He glanced at my notepad and cleared his throat again. "Not that that needs to be printed, of course. I only feel sympathy for their plight now." He shifted in his seat. "They couldn't have known that Panrose was taking advantage of them. I place the blame fully on the company, not the customers." His secretary poked her head in the door, and he waved her away with a frown.

"Naturally, naturally," I murmured. "And what led you to taking these tests on the water?"

"Concerned citizens contacted us," he puffed out his chest and pointed at me emphatically. "We have a reputation for honest dealings, you see. Honesty and integrity: that's Sero's highest priority with our customers."

"And they're not even your customers," I said dryly.

He looked taken aback and then recovered and nodded seriously. "It's our responsibility — all of us as members of this community — to look out for each other. That's all I'm trying to do. All I'm trying to do."

Felicity smiled at him, and he turned slightly pink.

"Mr. Gaines," I said, looking over my notes, "What is your history with the Hill community? Why look out for them?"

"Just as I've said, Miss Hopper, just a community member looking out for others. When I see fellow citizens being taken advantage of, I can't help but do something about it. Right the wrong."

"Can you tell us who contacted you for help?" I asked. "I'd like to follow up with them."

He shook his head slowly. "Sorry, so sorry. They came to me in strictest confidence. Didn't want it to come back on them." He shrugged and rubbed his fingers together.

"And what were they afraid of? What exactly would 'come back on them,' as you say?"

He sighed. "There are things in this world of business that you wouldn't understand. Not your fault at all; not your place, not your place. But these important people on the Hill can't risk going against the grain, you might say."

Holding back a sigh of my own, I said patiently, "The Franklin won't print their names, Mr. Gaines. I know how to handle a witness in danger of any kind. I'll use the utmost care."

He gave me a condescending smile and sat back in his chair; he was again rubbing his fingers. "I'm sorry. It wouldn't be right for me to betray their confidence, especially to a newspaperwoman."

I lifted my eyebrows. "I see."

"So loyal of you," Felicity breathed, leaning forward. "And completely understandable."

Gaines looked pleased. "I'm happy to help you in any way I can. There are just some lines I may not cross."

"What about the plans looked unsafe?" I asked.

"Their filtering system was completely inadequate," he answered after a pause, now rubbing his hand on his thigh. "The water source requires extensive purification. Some of the new parts that they use for such machinery will break down easily, letting more contaminants into the overflow. Other issues are quite complicated; I'm sure you understand…"

"And what did you do with this information once you found it?"

"Shared it with the Hill inhabitants, of course. And told the authorities. They were not interested." He shook his head sadly. "Sometimes public servants forget they are indeed servants of the public and not the other way around."

My limit of tolerance was topping out, but I scanned my notes for any further questions to help me later. "In the meantime, while this is being resolved, what would you recommend for the safety of the public? Boiling their water? Filtering it themselves?"

"Boiling it won't rid them of the contaminants. And

filtering it probably won't either. The best thing to do is bring the problem to Panrose in a way that is impossible for them to ignore."

"So that they can fix the machinery?"

"So they can shut it down! An entirely new generator will be necessary." He eyed us and then leaned forward earnestly. "And be sure to print that Sero Electric is here for all their needs as a concerned and reliable resource."

I gave him a tight smile and gathered my things, clicking off the autophone with a forceful little thwack.

"You've been ever so helpful," Felicity gushed, wringing his hand. "A real community hero, honest."

Gaines beamed as I hid a gag.

Once we were back on the street, Felicity was beaming, too.

"Are the cases always this easy?" she asked.

I studied her, trying to gauge her words. "No," I said. "Usually people are harder to read."

She nodded. "Makes sense. You'd think a man in his prominent position would have learned to lie better." Her flaming hair flew as she let out a peal of laughter. "Men can be so smarmy! What a grease can!" She imitated him rubbing his fingers and gave a quite realistic scowl. "You ignorant reporters wouldn't understand nothin'."

I allowed myself a small smile as we walked down the street. "You weren't so honest yourself back there." I didn't realize before I met her that eyes could hold so much gallivanting sparkle.

"Oh honey, you're a working girl. You know how to give them what they want to get them to talk. You just don't do it. Why not?"

I hid a smile as I considered her question. She reminded me of Ward, in that she had read quite a lot about me in a very short amount of time. "I suppose I don't care about telling people what they want to hear."

She shook her vibrant head. "I can't understand how you've made it this far in the newspaper biz. But you really are just the cats. This is great. I think we make the perfect team. By the by, you are going to teach me how to work that gizmo, aren't you?"

I handed over the autophone. "This gizmo is called an autophone, and yes, I'd love for you to do the recordings."

"Autophone? That doesn't look a bit like my old auntie's tiny organ."

I gave her a blank look. "Oh! The ones that run with punch cards?" I laughed a little. "I suppose Gene hadn't heard of those when he invented this. Look," I pointed, "that button there is the important one. You hold it down to record the voices that need to be picked up by the 'phone. Then you press this one here to start the interview."

She scratched her ear, eying the autophone. "Why two buttons? Why not just record?"

I shivered involuntarily, remembering. "The purpose of this is to catch only the voices you want on the recording. It filters out the background."

"Ingenious." She was apparently impressed into silence.

I nodded, trying to keep my mind on the present instead of returning to that fateful night at the hospital that still made my blood run cold and my throat rub hoarse from the screaming nightmares. "Yes, it is," I said.

She was watching me carefully, and I realized I had underestimated Felicity Jacks. She was much too intelligent for secrets.

"Was it his? Your former assistant's?"

I coughed, surprised again. "His invention, yes."

Her eyes widened. "His invention. This is a story I really need to hear someday. Don't worry, not today. I know a wounded person when I see one." She expertly dodged a bicyclist as we crossed the street. "But in the meantime, how about that guy?" She hitched her green purse up on her shoulder and jabbed her thumb behind us. "Where do we go next to disprove his baloney?"

Relieved to ponder the job instead of my startlingly insightful new assistant, I took my paper from my vest pocket and jotted down a couple of notes for the future. I'd need to contact some chemists — from a different company if necessary — and follow up on Gaines' dubious explanation of the generator plans. "I say we head directly to Panrose to learn more about the generator."

"We're certain that it's all perfect nonsense, right?"

I pocketed the notepad with a wry smile. "The tests? Yes. The 'concerned citizen source'? Yes. All his talk about the filtering system and overflow? Likely. But being certain after one interview isn't enough. I can be reasonably sure he's lying without being sure that the generator isn't dangerous. We need more information, especially about the sickness, which I've heard from my own source is legitimate, and if it is, we need to investigate the supposed 'logical' correlation. Whether or not this generator is tied to the epidemic, we have a lot to investigate." I paused, thinking. "I'm really quite interested in this story," I admitted.

Felicity actually rubbed her hands together with glee. "Can I do the recording?"

ABOUT THE AUTHOR

Britney Dehnert is a writer, poet, teacher, and mom. She's one half of the creative team behind the Ginnie Harper Mysteries, the Epoch Mythos series, and the Dark Moon trilogy (coming soon). The other half is her husband, J.P., who brainstorms with her, plots and outlines the stories, and creates covers and fan fun. Britney and J.P. make their home wherever they happen to be at the moment with their two daughters. They love blanket forts, pizza picnics in the living room, exploration from the backyard to distant planets, wardrobes that lead to fantasy lands, and road trips.

You can read more from them on their website, www.britneydehnertbooks.com/sneakpeeks

ACKNOWLEDGMENTS

This story was written the most rapidly of my books, and it also marked the beginning of a very special partnership between my husband and I. Thank you, babe, for striking out on this venture with me — I love you more every day.

My sister Janelle and friend Amanda, thank you for reading along with me even as we changed plot points halfway through! Your encouragement has been vital.

My parents, my first full-book readers, thank you for reading all my other books, even the fantasy ones.

To my pearl of a mom-in-law, and one of my best friends, thank you for the gift of your time. You stood guard over nap time and played with our babies while I gallivanted off into Ginnie's world to write her story, and I'll forever be grateful. This trilogy would have taken much longer to write without you.

Steve and Clair, thank you for the tour through the physical space of the *Riverton Ranger* and the tour through the mind of a reporter. You gave both the *Franklin Journal* and Ginnie Harper new insights and reality. Clair, I'm honored that you brought me into your world so I could make Ginnie's world better, and I'm grateful beyond words to have gained your friendship in the process.

Amber, a fellow author and new friend, who gave me incredibly helpful feedback and got me started on a research path that led to so much richness both in my career and personal life, thank you.

Dr. Kevin Smith, thank you for agreeing to read my manuscript and check it for historical inaccuracies: your feedback was thoughtful and insightful, not only for the time period of the text but also for the sake of the story itself.

All my readers, especially you who show me my typos, write honest reviews, and email me encouragement: I appreciate you beyond words. Thank you for coming on this journey with me.

ALSO BY BRITNEY DEHNERT

Ginnie Harper Staticpunk Mysteries

The Truth in the Dark

The Truth in the Water

The Truth in the Vault

Epoch Mythos Series (for Fantasy fans)

Journey of the Maple

Anchor Between Worlds

Prayer Poetry

A NICU Mama's Journey in Prayer

A Tired Mama's Journey in Prayer

A Toddler Mama's Journey in Prayer

See www.britneydehnertbooks.com for all books and blog posts by
Britney Dehnert